LUTHER: FIRST OF THE FALLEN

Further reading from The Horus Heresy

THE HORUS HERESY®

Book 1 – HORUS RISING
Dan Abnett

Book 2 – FALSE GODS
Graham McNeill

Book 3 – GALAXY IN FLAMES
Ben Counter

Book 4 – THE FLIGHT OF
THE EISENSTEIN
James Swallow

THE HORUS HERESY®
SIEGE OF TERRA

Book 1 – THE SOLAR WAR
John French

Book 2 – THE LOST AND
THE DAMNED
Guy Haley

Book 3 – THE FIRST WALL
Gav Thorpe

Book 4 – SATURNINE
Dan Abnett

Book 5 – MORTIS
John French

Book 6 – WARHAWK
Chris Wraight

Book 7 – ECHOES OF ETERNITY
Aaron Dembski-Bowden

Book 8 – THE END AND THE DEATH:
VOLUME I
Dan Abnett

Book 8 – THE END AND THE DEATH:
VOLUME II
Dan Abnett

Book 8 – THE END AND THE DEATH:
VOLUME III
Dan Abnett

SONS OF THE SELENAR (Novella)
Graham McNeill

FURY OF MAGNUS (Novella)
Graham McNeill

GARRO: KNIGHT OF GREY (Novella)
James Swallow

THE HORUS HERESY®
PRIMARCHS

ANGRON:
SLAVE OF NUCERIA
Ian St. Martin

KONRAD CURZE:
THE NIGHT HAUNTER
Guy Haley

LION EL'JONSON:
LORD OF THE FIRST
David Guymer

ALPHARIUS:
HEAD OF THE HYDRA
Mike Brooks

The Horus Heresy Character Series

VALDOR:
BIRTH OF THE IMPERIUM
Chris Wraight

LUTHER:
FIRST OF THE FALLEN
Gav Thorpe

SIGISMUND:
THE ETERNAL CRUSADER
John French

EIDOLON:
THE AURIC HAMMER
Marc Collins

*Order the full range of Horus Heresy novels, audio dramas and audiobooks
from blacklibrary.com*

LUTHER: FIRST OF THE FALLEN

GAV THORPE

A BLACK LIBRARY PUBLICATION

First published in 2020.
This edition published in Great Britain in 2025 by
Black Library, Games Workshop Ltd., Willow Road,
Nottingham, NG7 2WS, UK.
Represented by: Games Workshop Limited – Irish branch,
Unit 3, Lower Liffey Street, Dublin 1,
D01 K199, Ireland.

10 9 8 7 6 5 4 3 2 1

Produced by Games Workshop in Nottingham.
Cover illustration by Anna Lakisova.

Luther: First of the Fallen © Copyright Games Workshop Limited
2025. Luther: First of the Fallen, GW, Games Workshop, Black
Library, The Horus Heresy, The Horus Heresy Eye logo, Space Marine,
40K, Warhammer, Warhammer 40,000, the 'Aquila' Double-headed
Eagle logo, and all associated logos, illustrations, images, names,
creatures, races, vehicles, locations, weapons, characters, and the
distinctive likenesses thereof, are either ® or TM, and/or © Games
Workshop Limited, variably registered around the world.
All Rights Reserved.

A CIP record for this book is available from the British Library.

ISBN 13: 978-1-83609-152-3

No part of this publication may be reproduced, stored in a retrieval
system, or transmitted in any form or by any means, electronic,
mechanical, photocopying, recording or otherwise, without the
prior permission of the publishers.

This is a work of fiction. All the characters and events portrayed
in this book are fictional, and any resemblance to real people or
incidents is purely coincidental.

See Black Library on the internet at

blacklibrary.com

Find out more about Games Workshop
and the worlds of Warhammer at

warhammer.com

Printed and bound in the UK.

Dedicated to Jervis Johnson, who first chronicled the ill fate of Caliban.

It is a time of legend.

Mighty heroes battle for the right to rule the galaxy. The vast armies of the Emperor of Mankind conquer the stars in a Great Crusade – the myriad alien races are to be smashed by His elite warriors and wiped from the face of history.

The dawn of a new age of supremacy for humanity beckons. Gleaming citadels of marble and gold celebrate the many victories of the Emperor, as system after system is brought back under His control. Triumphs are raised on a million worlds to record the epic deeds of His most powerful champions.

First and foremost amongst these are the primarchs, superhuman beings who have led the Space Marine Legions in campaign after campaign. They are unstoppable and magnificent, the pinnacle of the Emperor's genetic experimentation, while the Space Marines themselves are the mightiest human warriors the galaxy has ever known, each capable of besting a hundred normal men or more in combat.

Many are the tales told of these legendary beings. From the halls of the Imperial Palace on Terra to the outermost reaches of Ultima Segmentum, their deeds are known to be shaping the very future of the galaxy. But can such souls remain free of doubt and corruption forever? Or will the temptation of greater power prove too much for even the most loyal sons of the Emperor?

The seeds of heresy have already been sown, and the start of the greatest war in the history of mankind is but a few years away…

TALE OF THE LONG NIGHT

He remembered the world breaking.

It was very confused; everything happened at the same time, a kaleidoscope of images, conflicting and noisy. The sky burned. No, not burned. A storm. A storm not of this reality, devouring the universe.

The gods had claimed their dues.

He had not expected anything quite so… apocalyptic.

Pain broke into his thoughts. Intense. Sharp.

A blade lanced into his side and he screamed.

He screamed at the memory of it. It was not in his side any longer. He could feel the wound, raw and bleeding. It mirrored the wound in the sky that had swallowed his army.

The hand that had driven the blade, inhumanly strong. Stronger even than he was. Stronger than the archaic technologies that had given him such endurance and long life. Stronger than the will of the gods.

Driven by hate that had burned in eyes the green of Caliban's forests.

Caliban's lost forests…

So long ago.

Eyes of a demigod, filled with rage.

A heartbeat. A thunderous heartbeat, drumming, drumming. His own? Why couldn't he see? He had the memory of sight, but he was in darkness. They had fixed his eyes. He could see as well as a wildcat at night and a hawk in the day. One of the simplest procedures, but one of the most effective. How did one see the world as he did? What did the universe look like to a creature made of science and myth?

The drumming was not his heart. That slowly and surely resounded in his chest. He felt the pulse of it in the blood vessels in his neck, at his temples, throbbing through wrist and thigh. He had never been so aware of his body.

The drumming was footfalls. Quick strides thudding on rock.

Eyes made perfect by the arcane knowledge of the Dark Age finally adjusted to the gloom, picking out the slightest of light sources, sketching in broken ruins. A toppled statue lay to his left, of a knightly figure with blade held in salute, snapped at the waist. An archway had collapsed behind him.

Lights approached, a pair of lamps moving up and down in time with the foot-drums. Less than two hundred metres away, several metres lower than where he lay upon the slope of a tumbled wall.

His hearing had also been honed to preternatural accuracy and he detected another sound amidst the trickling of grit and dust, the patter of liquid from a ruptured pipe and the creak of settling masonry. The sound was a mechanical wheeze. As the lights grew brighter and brighter they brought with them a hum of electrical circuitry too.

The suit lamps dimmed, their illumination replaced by a

sudden cerulean brightness that caused him to flinch. The movement sent a stab of pain crackling up through pulped ribs, searing through the coagulating wound in his flank.

The blue light flickered as a flame for several seconds before assuming the shape of an axe blade, forming a crackling field around the weapon. It was impossible to tell the colour of the armour in the harsh light. Dark, but black or green?

Smell.

Sweat. A lot of blood. His own, most likely. The residue of bolter rounds and ozone aftertaste of las and plasma discharge. Smells of battle. Smells he had learned as a child.

Lubricant, alien and strong. Not the maintenance oils used by the Order but something else. The approaching figure was not of this world. Martian smells.

One of the demigod's warriors.

The Space Marine stopped at the bottom of the steep rubble slope, one booted foot crunching onto the shattered brick. He leaned forward, the light of the axe revealing a scarred face with trifurcated beard and a dark stubble breaking a bald scalp. The eyes widened with shock.

'Luther.'

His name brought further clarity. Names had power and his brought him back to the present in a way that the barbs of broken stone in his spine had not. The voice was familiar, but the face was a mystery at first. The thud of other footsteps echoed behind the stranger as he slowly processed what he was looking at. Not one of the Order, one of the Dark Angels. A face he had not seen for more than five decades. He removed the scars, mentally healing the ravages of wars both old and recent, until he could place the features.

'Farith?' His voice was little more than a croaking whisper. 'Wait… I need to–'

The warrior took a step.

'Bastard traitor!'

Blue light blazed as the axe swung.

Harsh edges of metal brought him round, biting at wrists and ankles. He was in irons, chained to a chair. He had been stripped of his armour's remnants and was clad in a stiff kilt of leather, such as one might train in when unarmed. The pain in his side was no more. Paralysis? His heart thudded at the thought, but the ache of the shackles on his legs proved the falseness of the theory.

He had been healed, then. By whom?

Opening his eyes revealed the face he last remembered before the axe had struck him. The flat of it, given that he still lived. The Paladin, Farith. One of the last to be squired to the Order by the Lion before the First Legion had arrived. He was a cold killer; Luther had disliked him but admired his ruthlessness, and he was utterly dedicated to the Lion. It was hard to reconcile the clean-cheeked youth with the haggard soldier in front of him. The years had not been kind.

Farith was also unarmoured, clad in a heavy sleeveless robe of dark green, embellished only with the Legion symbol upon the left breast – a downward-pointing sword flanked by wings, in thick white thread. They both sat in a chamber just a few metres square, furnished only with the two chairs. Something moved in the shadows beyond the door. Red eyes gleamed inside a dark hood, the height of a small child's face, but Luther knew it was no infant. A Watcher in the Dark. It had been some time since he had laid eyes upon one of Caliban's mysterious guardians. It was gone a heartbeat later.

'Where is the Lion?' asked Farith, leaning forward, thick forearms resting on his knees.

The question surprised Luther. His side spasmed as though the sword were still buried there. The room swirled in and out of focus, merging with flashes of memory and sights of what had not yet arrived. The storm that had engulfed them, that had swept up his warriors, now swirled inside his thoughts. With an effort he broke out of its nebulous grip, blinking as he focused on the legionary before him.

Luther was sure that there was something he was supposed to do, or say, but he could not recall it. Farith asked the question again, more forcefully.

'I do not know what happened to the Lion. Aldurukh broke. We fell. He is not with you?'

Farith shook his head, eyes fixed on Luther. There was barely suppressed fury in that gaze.

'Caliban...' Farith looked away, jaw clenched. He was shaking, hands making fists and unclenching. The robe stretched as he took in a long breath and looked once more at his prisoner. 'Caliban is no more. It was destroyed by the bombardment and warp storm. There is no sign of the primarch. Tell me what you remember.'

'Little,' confessed Luther, frowning. 'My thoughts twist into themselves, more contorted than a forest path. Past, present, future. I wander among them. I cannot tell one from the other. Have we had this conversation before?'

'Where did you send your followers?'

'Send?' Luther recalled the storm, tendrils of warp power flashing down, striking like lightning. 'I sent them nowhere. They were taken. The storm! I remember what happened now. In shadow, at least. The storm. I had to get to the heart. The Lion and I... He stopped me before I could stop it. I needed to... I cannot recall. It was important, but the Lion... We fought, but I did not kill him. I would not.'

Farith sat back as he absorbed this, eyes narrowing in suspicion. 'You protest innocence?'

'I did not summon the storm, I did not kill the Lion,' Luther assured him. Farith's words filtered through the tumult of his mind, settling like debris on the shore of his thoughts. He looked around the cell, confused. 'Caliban is no more?'

Farith nodded.

'Broken by your sorcery and the guns of the fleet. Aldurukh's energy fields sustain the tower, the rest is rock and ash scattered across the void.'

'No, you are lying,' said Luther. 'I saved Caliban from destruction. I saw it. Or not. It is still moving, the fog and the storm.'

Panic set in, speeding his heart, sweating his palms as the notion took root. Farith said nothing, offering no word of defence.

'I saved Caliban,' Luther said again, but as he spoke his words fell quieter with doubt. 'I saved Caliban...'

He was going to save Caliban. Was that it? Or save the Lion? Was it memory or something else?

'You doomed Caliban.' Farith's sneer was more cutting than any sword edge. 'You betrayed the Lion and destroyed our world.'

'No, that was not how it happened,' protested Luther. He tried to rise but the restraints bit into flesh and bone as he struggled. 'No! He betrayed me! He abandoned us!'

Luther slumped into the chair, chains rattling, frustrated as Farith just glowered at him in silence. The storm. Everything breaking. The fall. Like the depths that had swallowed him and the Lion, his gut became a deep chasm.

Hollow, emptied out like a swine's carcass for the roasting spit. As empty as the oaths he had taken. Oaths he had thrown away for... For what? It was hard to remember.

'You killed the Lion and destroyed Caliban,' said Farith, every word heavy with the weight of its accusation.

Luther raised no argument, letting the charges settle on him like a shroud. His mouth was dry, his bones ached and yet the greatest discomfort was the knowledge that Farith spoke the truth. Not about the Lion, but about Caliban's fate. The planet of his birth was no more. He had tried to bring it back, to restore it to the way it was meant to be, but he had failed.

And he had dishonoured himself and the Order. For nothing. For lies and vainglory.

'Are those tears, traitor?' Farith grimaced, standing up. 'You do not get to shed tears. You are not allowed sorrow for what you have done.'

Luther choked back his grief and nodded, acknowledging the right of Farith's anger.

'I… I was weak,' he began.

I was weak when I thought I was being strong.

A moment was fast approaching when our fates would be set. Whose fates do I mean? Myself and my council, a mixture of disparate souls that had found common cause in our secession from the Imperium. Once we had been united under the auspices of the Legion, now we were bonded by something even stronger: mutual need.

My seneschal was perhaps the most unlikely of candidates, not even born of Caliban. The Terran veteran Sar Astelan, who bore a grudge against the Lion greater than any other of us. Astelan was my commander openly, and in secret he was my chief of espionage, enforcement and the other unpleasantries of rule. Our arrangement was simple but effective: he was loyal to me and I asked no questions about his business or what he did to maintain my authority and that of the Order.

My chief advisor was a companion of long acquaintance who had never been a Dark Angel direct, but by dint of her associations with command of the Order had benefited from the physical enhancements gifted to me and the other senior knights when the Emperor arrived. We were too old to become legionaries, but there were plenty of augmetics and bio-therapies that could still be applied to make us formidable, long-lived warriors. She was Saulus Maegon, the deadly mistress of the Angelicasta, who had been in command of Caliban's greatest fortress for decades.

Then there was Sar Griffayn, the Spear-Cast, formerly the voted lieutenant of the Firewing. A traditionalist who had been returned to us on a fleet of ships sent for reinforcements and, following the death of their leader, Belath, come over to our cause along with the survivors of a brief but bloody internecine fight. His defection was perhaps the most important and heartening, for he had not been one of us isolated on Caliban and yet still saw the worth in our goals for autonomy. Inculcated in the oldest rites of the Legion, nevertheless his loyalty was to Caliban over the Dark Angels. It had boded well that we might encounter others who would lend ear to our arguments, and that those arguments came from one of such standing in the Legion gave them some weight outside of the Order.

Finally, there could be no council of the Order without the Lord Cypher. Guardian of our history and judge of our current character, the Lord Cypher was a figure steeped in the tradition of Aldurukh and Caliban and no Grand Master would have legitimacy without him. For us there was additional benefit to his inclusion, for my Lord Cypher had before been the Librarian Zahariel, a psyker, and so doubled as the master of my Mystai.

This was my council, the leaders of Caliban beneath me, the Grand Master of the Order.

Our great endeavour was now poised upon glory or ruin, our striving for independence about to face the final test of strength.

The Lion.

He was returning after many decades of fighting the battles of the Emperor. The massive war fleet of the First, the honoured Dark Angels, was but days or even hours from breaking warp at the edge of the system. Lord Cypher and our own warp auguries had confirmed as much, for so many ships do not travel unannounced through the immaterium. We had flotillas of our own: some won through guile and conquest; others raised in the shipyards of Zaramund, which we had made our colony; yet more supplied from other worlds that had been brought within the ruling sphere of Caliban.

The star system was a fortress yet to be tested, and the strength of the Lion was not certain. Yet always the advantage is with the defender, and so we were confident that if it came to martial examination we would not be found the weaker.

Not in military terms, at least.

It was Astelan that first raised concern when the council was convened. I remember it clearly. We met in the Chamber of Arthorus as we often did, lit by the early sun. Morning training had commenced and the noise of feigned combat rang through the open window from the mustering fields and shooting ranges beyond the Angelicasta.

'They are ready,' Maegon assured us. She and Astelan were jointly in charge of recruitment and training, combining the best rites and culture of the Order with the disciplines of the Legion we had left behind.

'Physically,' the Terran countered. He took fruit from the bowl on the table. A red apple, newly harvested from orchards on the western slopes. He did not take a bite but continued. 'In their minds, in their hearts, we cannot be sure.'

'Sure of what, Sar Astelan?' Griffayn asked. The voted lieutenant was my void-general, the most experienced starship commander among us, and would lead the defence beyond the surface. 'They are brave as any Space Marine can be.'

'I do not question their courage,' Astelan told us. He bit the apple and chewed for several seconds, brow furrowed, before speaking again. 'I am sure they will face the blades and bolts of our foes without a moment's hesitation. But we can't say for sure if they will fight back.'

'Their loyalty is to the Order,' said Maegon. She looked at me, her tone insistent. 'Every doctrine they know reinforces their allegiance to Aldurukh, to Caliban and to you.'

I rewarded her with a smile of confidence, for I knew of what Astelan spoke and it was no accusation against the mistress of the Angelicasta.

'All is as I have required, Sarl Maegon,' I assured her. 'Their older companions have proven skilful on battlefields already and I have no doubt in their competence. But Sar Astelan's point is correct. To be loyal is one matter. To turn blades against the Dark Angels, some of them Calibanites, is a different matter.'

Astelan's concerns were a veiled question for me to answer. Always had our alliance been uneasy, our mutuality uncertain. His hatred for the Lion outweighed his attested loyalty to the Emperor Himself. If he was not willing to accuse me openly, I decided to answer in likewise oblique fashion.

'There are those in the ranks that have already spilled the blood of the Dark Angels,' I reminded him. 'Veterans from the events in the Hall of Decemial. They are our lieutenants now, under Sar Griffayn.'

'Two dozen, perhaps,' added Lord Cypher. 'Myself counted among those that executed the assassins in our midst.'

'Two dozen among tens of thousands?' scoffed Astelan. 'I agree that they will give the order, but will fingers tighten on triggers, will swords leave sheaths on their word?'

'You have picked the recruits and trained them, but you do not understand the nature of your army,' I told Astelan, wearied by his arguments. 'These are not legionaries of the Emperor fighting other legionaries. Save for a heart of former First like yourself, warriors who have proven their worth and loyalty already, the others are knights of the Order. They have sworn oaths only to me and to our institution.'

It was surprisingly Lord Cypher that made plainer the interrogation behind Astelan's questions.

'Will the order be given, Grand Master?' he asked me directly. 'All has been arranged with you at the centre. Without your command, our war for independence will end.'

'Yes, Sar Luther,' said Griffayn. 'We stand as a weapon loaded but it is your finger upon the trigger.'

I raised eyebrows at how swiftly my lieutenants gathered about this theme against me. It was less of a shock that Astelan made more plain his unease with my command arrangements.

'At least give us the defence activation code,' he said. His tone was more demanding than I liked but I held my tongue. 'All of our systems are slaved to a single phrase that only you know, Sar Luther. The delay of communication could prove costly during the battle.'

I looked at them each with slow regard, keeping my temper in check. This was no time for divisions or authoritarianism. If just one of them chose the Lion over me we would all be undone. In a way it was gratifying. There was no bickering, no distrust among them for each other. Their only concern was in their commander, which was disappointing on a personal level. I needed to choose my words with care, so as not to gloat or bludgeon, but to remind them of the pertinent facts.

There was one last question I had to ask myself: Did I trust *them*?

'Caliban would still be a slave of the Emperor if not for me,' I told them quietly. I sat back in my chair, relaxed. 'I have been expecting this day for many years. We all have, but none for longer than me. Maegon, you and I alone remember Caliban before the Emperor, and perhaps yours was the even longer exile, condemned to remain in this fortress while the Legion departed for the Great Crusade. The rest of you are followers to the cause that I began, never forget that. We each have our reasons to be sat at this table now, but if Maegon has kept this fortress standing, it is by my will that it remains home to the Order alone. None of you could command the Order as I do, either by ability or tradition.'

I paused at that moment, giving them opportunity to gainsay my statement, for I wanted all debate to be aired then and not saved an hour longer.

Griffayn was the first to bow his head in acquiescence. Always obedient, what he had witnessed on the Great Crusade and in the fleet of Corswain had broken his faith in the Imperial cause – after I had highlighted the truth for him.

I thought Astelan would continue his argument, for he had no loyalty to the Order save for how it served his revenge against the Lion. But in this I found him the most trustworthy, of sorts, because he had no pretension to leadership or even Caliban's independence. The Order and our world was a means to an end and as long as I promised to deliver that end he was absolutely dedicated to our success.

He stayed silent, but his annoyance remained clear.

Lord Cypher steepled his fingers before him and looked at me for some time through the lenses of his helm. It mattered nothing that I had given him his position and knew the man within, he was Lord Cypher now and carried all the respect and authority that entailed. Had I done him disservice with my doubts?

'You are right, Sar Luther, that there is not another of us that could have created what we have here. I do not doubt your dedication to the Order. There is none that has done more in its long history to bring honour and glory to Aldurukh and no other I would entrust with its future.'

I expected some qualification or equivocation to follow, but none came. Lord Cypher clasped his hands together and nod-ded, satisfied with his input.

'I will think on what you have said,' I promised them, rising. 'We convene again in two hours, for the last conference before battle. I will give you my answer then.'

I left them to discuss whatever matters that required such conversation and returned to my chambers. They had been enlarged in recent years, expanded to encompass the sizeable library I had assembled. The core of it remained the books of the Knights of Lupus I had taken, which had first introduced me to the truth beyond the teachings of the Order and the Imperial Truth.

Yet I had outgrown those tomes in time, having drained them of all knowledge with much reading. With the aid of Zahariel and a few select others, I had acquired more works, from across Caliban and ultimately other worlds. My Lord Cypher never spoke of it, but he had to know the manner of the books I took from him, and I knew that his Mystai were far more than the Librarians of the Space Marines.

Such works were not to be kept lightly: harsh experience had taught me that precautions had to be taken with some of the volumes of deeper lore. So it was that the inner sanctum of my quarters more closely resembled a vault or arsenal than it did personal chambers, much reinforced by beams inscribed with potent charms, the heavy lead-lined door from my study locked not only with physical bonds but also enchantments of a pro-tective nature, taught to me by the Mystai and culled from the texts held within.

My dorm had become a place of only passing interest in the preceding years, for often I would study for days at a time, and when sleep finally crept upon me I would collapse in the cushioned chair behind my desk. I was always certain to retire from the library before too late in order that I remained of cogent enough mind to invoke the protections. The price of fatigue-induced carelessness would have been heavy indeed.

I see now that the library had gained more of a hold over me than I realised. Knowledge is powerful, but dangerous in obsession. And I had become obsessed. Not with knowledge for its own sake, but as a means to ensure the security and sanctity of Caliban against our coming foes. There were tracts that lingered in my mind long after their reading, and many are the nuggets of lore that fixed my thoughts and plagued my dreams for days or even weeks. I cannot recall any of them now, for they were ripped from my mind by the storm, even as it raged across our world.

And therein lies a lesson, I think. Knowledge only has power when earned, not freely imparted. At first I questioned the nature of what I read, what I was learning. The Knights of Lupus had protected their works for a reason and I similarly guarded against others, save the Mystai, learning what I possessed. Not honourable Griffayn, certainly not Astelan. And I would not inflict such a burden upon Maegon, oldest of my allies.

Upon returning that morning, after the council, I passed into the inner sanctum having prepared the wards for my passage and secured the outer chamber against intrusion by a subordinate, as I had done hundreds, thousands of times before. Always I was careful to be mindful of these actions, not to conduct them out of rote. Presence of mind in all things, I counsel. Be aware of thyself before all else.

The inner sanctum was a small room, sealed with layers of ferrocrete, lead and titanium, the walls behind the shelves laced with sorcerous alloys. It pains me to say it, but the artisans that created the inner sanctum perished soon after, taking the knowledge of its existence to their unmarked graves. As I said, be careful from whom one gains knowledge and be aware of the price of its acquisition.

Not only to contain were those wards raised, but to shield from view. For as long as records have been made, Aldurukh had been home to the creatures we called the Watchers in the Dark. Of late they had abandoned coming directly, seen only on the edge of vision, at the moment of sleep or waking, in the shadows of the last and first light. They remained but their scorn was palpable. Now suspicious of their intent, I sought to keep from their knowledge all that passed within my library.

Ha! But I speak wisely now, though as a fool I was. More clearly with the telling does this lesson become one I should have heard many years ago.

Within the inner sanctum the floor was cleared and upon it were carved symbols of summoning and containment, to channel and manifest the energies of the immaterium. Other accoutrements were set about a circle, which enclosed a pentagon, which in turn held within it a triangle. Just as the spiral of our martial training creates a better, more focused warrior, so the concentric wards honed the power of entreatment.

Within the triangle waited one of the nephilla. I learned many names for such creatures, but it was by the Calibanite term that I always titled them. Nephilla, spirits not of the mortal world. Even on a planet of fantastic beasts and semi-living forests the nephilla were something of a dubious subject, particularly after the coming of the Imperium's servants and the brutal imposition of rationality and suppression of our traditional beliefs.

This particular specimen was my primary contact with the World Beyond, as I was wont to call the empyrean and all lands of the powers not of mortal origin. Its true name had been erased, but for my own benefit I called it a bastardised version in conversation: Ezqurol. Its form was impermanent as any denizen of the immaterial realm, but it favoured the aspect of a small, grumpy creature with flesh of blue flame. When I entered it was sitting with its back to me upon the charred planks of its containment, grumbling loudly in a language I could not understand. Wherever I walked in the chamber it appeared to be facing away from me.

It was almost laughable, infantile, but I knew better than to underestimate this creature. It quested always to be free of its imprisonment, either by being dismissed or by breaking its bonds. It had occasionally succeeded in the first and only been closely thwarted in the second. Today it was trying to be uncooperative, having delivered its message from the power that had conjured it into being at my request. Alas I cannot recall the identity of its creator in any detail now, even by allegory, save to recall a title: the Master of Magic. This herald had become my regular, though not sole, conduit to the powers that live beyond our realm.

'You said that one of them would betray me,' I said to it, coming to the lectern of black-lacquered wood that held open the volume to which I had been referring before the council. 'You lied.'

'*Cannot lie,*' the creature said between more unintelligible complaints. '*Bound by hex and word.*'

'But you will not tell me which one is the traitor,' I said to it, as I traced through the lines of the conjuration on the open pages. I found what I was looking for, a few lines of text that would elicit a pained reaction from Ezqurol when spoken aloud.

I spoke them aloud.

'*Stop it!*' it snarled at me. '*No lies!*'

'Perhaps I will keep you here instead, doing nothing at all.' It changed form, rearranging itself without moving as such so that it was standing facing me, small flickers of fists raised in anger. I began to recite the words of punishment again and it screeched at me to stop.

'*No more! Relent! Mercy!*'

'Tell me again of the traitor,' I said, as I stepped from the lectern, careful not to pass the outer bounds of the summoning ring. 'Word by word, repeat what you said before.'

'You asked if all on your council were sound,' cackled the creature, as it showed rare mirth at my earlier moment of doubt. I had indeed consulted it to determine if it knew of any of my commanders moving against me. A precaution, fuelled by a paranoia made keen by the approaching confrontation.

It started to hum tunelessly, but soon a rhythm entered, in time with pulsing of its flames from deep blue to bright azure.

> *'In Aldurukh, in shadows cold,*
> *Where before the knights of old,*
> *Had gathered in their pomp and glory,*
> *Now is told a different story.'*

The nephilla started to pirouette slowly, stretching out its arms as it continued, droplets of fire falling from its fingertips.

> *'Conspirators, a clandestine meeting,*
> *Veiled in darkness, silent greeting.*
> *A lord to slay, their words unspoken,*
> *Payment taken for oaths long broken.*

> *'And in their quiet confiding,*
> *Another traitor smugly hiding,*
> *To turn upon turncoats at the last,*
> *And right the wrongs of distant past.*

> *'Truth is lost in blind ambition,*
> *When loyalty gives way to grand suspicion,*
> *And allies seek that which is gone,*
> *Repent too late, the damage done.'*

Its voice dropped to a gleeful whisper, eyes of bright sparks fixed upon me, a cruel smile showing teeth of silver needles.

'All dreams must fail in passing time,
Hope is lost with bell's last chime.
The lie to which your sons have striven,
Will forever remain the unforgiven.'

The creature of flame fell silent, glowering at me again from beneath brows of fire, fingers tapping tip to tip as it watched me, each contact like the flare of a match head.

The verse was the sort of vagueness I had come to expect from the messengers of the empyrean powers, and yet I knew from study, and the bindings I had placed upon Ezqurol, that they were neither random nor without aid. The warning was within them, but purposefully veiled.

'Your advice is too generic!' I complained, having listened to the words again. I had first heard them before dawn and pondered them until the meeting, hoping their meaning would be revealed by something that occurred during the council.

I had nothing more to help with deciphering the rhyme, and I wondered for some time whether it referred to a secret cabal not aligned with my council at all, though Astelan assured me that there was no resistance to our command anywhere on Caliban.

My next thought was for the Lord Cypher, and more specifically his Mystai. They had access to ancient texts that told of mysteries even older than those found in the Library of Lupus. Certainly Zahariel, as he had been, had shown himself capable of following his own agenda at times, but both my own reasoning and the probes of Astelan had found nothing to suggest that they would benefit from the failure of our endeavour.

Such is the nature of conspiracy and resistance. The needs of the one quickly become the needs of all. One cannot gain one's own victories apart from the others, and so all goals becomes the same goal.

After that…?

Many a rebellion fails in the aftermath, when the enemy is overthrown and a new regime must reign. Was that the nature of Ezqurol's warning? I thought. When the Lion was defeated, our common foe would be gone.

Certainly Astelan owed me nothing beyond that point. If any was the first to turn, it would be the Terran. But he lacked a power base. The few followers he had that I judged loyal to him before Caliban were imprisoned beneath the tower of the Angelicasta, and ranged against the strength of the Order they were too few to usurp power by force alone.

Over and over I cast each of my companions as the villain, trying to discern motive for their abandonment and the means by which it would transpire. I came up with nothing convincing, and not only because I offered more to them than continued service to the Lion or the Emperor. Each had a personal reason to see the task to its completion and to support the transition after.

As my frustration grew, so Ezqurol grew more animated, pacing its incorporeal prison, glaring and spitting.

If I could not trust all of my council, I could trust none of them. It was far too late in our plans to reform the inner circle.

I sensed impatience from my immaterial captive.

'It is doubt!' I shouted in triumph, rounding on the creature. It hissed in annoyance by way of reply. 'Doubt, suspicion, uncertainty. They are the traitors in the dark counsels of our thoughts! Repent too late, the damage done! You think I will stay my hand, hold back the command when the time comes too.'

'*You have proven your weakness already,*' it said with a scowl. '*You have your answer, let me be!*'

'I am not weak,' I replied, and it was then that I committed the grave offence of listening to my ego. 'The verse was about me? You call me traitor to my own cause?'

'*The architect knows best the flaws in his plans,*' Ezqurol replied. '*The chain breaks at its weakest point. The ambition you harbour will devour you, mortal.*'

'I lead for Caliban,' I declared, and in my rash mood I raised my fist, and in doing so my foot parted the outer ward of the binding hexes.

Ezqurol needed no further invite and hurled itself at me, a bolt of blue flame that surged up my leg, escaping the ring of containment.

Afire with sorcerous energy, I fell backwards, my shout held fast by the thick walls. Ezqurol formed into a semblance of its usual self, dancing upon my chest, singeing its footprints into my robe and flesh while it cackled a song of victory.

I swept out an arm but my warding limb passed through it with just a flutter of its fiery body.

'*Free!*' it screeched in my face, setting fingers of cerulean flame around my throat.

But I was not without a measure of sorcerous ability. The teachings of the Imperium would have you believe that it requires a freak of birth to make one a psyker, but my readings had revealed the lie of that. With practice and rite, one can open doors to strengthen the mind and access the powers that some can wield by mutation.

I summoned that energy now, cladding my fists in wreaths of lightning as I struck again, flinging the nephilla across the library. It exploded like a grenade against the ward-inscribed bookcase, wailing as it fell to the floor.

Quick as a cat it found its feet and this time, rather than

attack me, it sought to escape. It threw itself at the walls as though to pass the material barrier, but found in a flash and bang that they were barred in the immortal plane also. In desperation it bounded to the ceiling, and scrambled above me moaning as runes burned its hands and feet with sanctuary force.

I turned and cornered it as it rebounded from the door charms, its fiery form laced through with tendrils of black and red as it flailed across the room.

I let streams of lightning rip from my fingertips, but it darted forward as quick as a las-blast, leaping for the lectern that held the spell which had bound it. I curbed my power for fear that destroying the tome might break what remained of the spell tying Ezqurol to the chamber.

The pages fluttered before it, its sparking eyes scanning the text, as I raced across the room. The fiend gave a triumphant cry just as my fingers, anointed with black fire, gripped its flaming limb and heaved it away. It rammed fingertips of fire into my face, blinding me, and in pain I cried out the words of unbinding I had committed to memory, while I hurled the creature back to the centre of the pentangle-bonds.

I heard a crack like thunder and the air smelt fresh and bright as in the aftermath of an electrical storm.

It took some time for my sight to recover, and my vision was still blurred when the occasion came for the council to next convene. While I donned my armour and hooded robe to conceal my wounds I pondered why the creature and its master had tried to undermine me. With the Lion defeated and Caliban free, did they fear I would turn from them? Or perhaps it was a final test of my resolve.

I would not be tricked. There would be no hesitation or discord.

'Starfire,' I announced when all were gathered again in the

Hall of Arthorus. 'Starfire is the word that will set the sky of Caliban alight.'

'I once thought you the greatest of us,' whispered Farith. 'None of us could be the Lion, just as a hen will never be an eagle. But you were raised a mortal like me, a paragon that could be emulated, a measure that could be matched. Yet you were the worst of us, and forgot everything you had been in one moment of vanity.'

'Vanity?' Luther shook his head. 'Is it vanity to recognise injustice? Was I vain to hope there could be a better future for my world?'

'Vanity clouded your hearing, when the nephilla spoke truth perhaps for the only time. You were the traitor, Luther. It has never been about Caliban, it was always about you. I have seen the powers of the warp so closely these last years, but I remained strong. I rejected them. Nothing good comes of their patronage, but you accepted it all the same. You needed it because you knew you were weak and when you failed them, they took it all from you. Your army, your knowledge. Your soul…?'

Luther stared at his interrogator, eyes brimming with moisture. All of it was true, and the verse of Ezqurol returned to him, but this time the words were like sparkling diamonds of clarity. His lips moved almost silently as he spoke them again.

'Repent too late, the damage done…' With trembling hand, he reached out to Farith. 'I am sorry.'

'You have slain the only one whose forgiveness might release you,' Farith growled. '"The lie to which your sons have striven will forever remain the unforgiven." You were warned but did not listen. Deaf to both mortal and immortal, your fate was sealed.'

'Wait!' cried Luther as Farith turned away. 'There is still time to learn. We are not yet doomed. Listen to me!'

The Paladin did not look back, and as the door swung shut Luther saw the glitter of red eyes in the dark.

TALE OF THE BEAST

Reality jarred, the last resounding thud of the door ending suddenly, and in the room before Luther stood another man. He was dressed in similar garb to Farith, darker of skin and hair. A scar twisted the left side of his upper lip, giving him a permanent sneer, and bionics pierced the same side of his scalp, metal glinting amid the short hair. He smelt of gun oil and incense.

The door was open behind him when moments before it had been slammed shut.

'What…?' Luther struggled as his senses crammed full of information like a starving man coming upon a feast.

Not only were his senses strained, his mind fluttered with strange images too. Memories? He certainly experienced flashes of the past. Faces from a previous life. Some he recognised, many he did not. Visions of Aldurukh and green forests whirled together.

But it was more than recollections that filled his thoughts. There were scenes he knew had not yet come to pass. Alien structures and abominable monsters stuttered through his broken mind, each a fresh horror. Blood spatters and the howl of mad warriors, the stench of rotting death and crash of tumbling walls. But that was Aldurukh again, was it not? Like the sacred spiral, symbol of Caliban and the centre of the Order's training, his tumultuous thought processes circled themselves again and again.

He started to speak, forcing himself to focus on the Space Marine in the chamber with him, even as his visitor turned back towards the door.

'Where is–'

The legionary disappeared and the door was closed again.

It creaked open and the man stepped through. His hair was longer, chin and cheeks stubbled with darkness. The dislocation made Luther dizzy and he hung his head in his hands, trying to stop the cell from spinning. His fingers traced the creases in his face, trying to recognise himself through touch alone. The former Grand Master of the Order rubbed his eyes and looked up, half expecting the stranger to have disappeared. He had not, but stood as he had done before, arms folded, glaring at his captive.

This time Luther did not struggle against the fluctuating barrage of memories and visions. He rode them, allowing them to wash around him, to carry him to their destination. It might have been moments or hours, it was impossible for Luther to tell, when the surge of conflicting plateaux finished their segues into each other.

'Luther.'

He looked up at mention of his name. There was something familiar about the man, despite his sudden change in appearance. Luther rubbed his chin in thought and it came to him. A name. A youth of the Order. No, of the Dark Angels. One of the last recruits that had been sent to the Lion before Zaramund and the true exile.

'Castagon?'

The Space Marine stiffened and his eyes narrowed.

'My name is Puriel now. Castagon is no more. I am Supreme Grand Master of the Dark Angels.'

'Where is Farith?'

'Dead.' Again the Space Marine's demeanour betrayed his unease. 'Dead for some thirty years.'

'A good death, I hope. With honour. In battle.'

'Slain by a traitor,' growled Puriel. 'One of your traitors, in fact.'

Luther rubbed at his brow, troubled by the assertion.

'The Order is no more. Farith said that Caliban was destroyed. My warriors were taken by the storm.'

'They were, but they were not slain by it. They survived the devastation.' Puriel unfolded his arms and flexed his fingers. 'Their confessions have been informative. Still, there is much we can learn only from the architects of the treachery. You were their leader. You took them along the path of corruption.'

The arguments sprang to mind again: the fight for freedom, from the tyranny of the Emperor. Caliban debased and consumed by a rapacious Imperium. Generations of children indentured to serve an indifferent lord or taken away to die in wars not of their making.

Excuses. Excuses for his weakness.

'The past is dead. You cannot resurrect it.' Luther stood up, causing Puriel to retreat a step, fists rising slightly. The leader of the Order checked his stride so that he did not approach, and clasped his hands behind his back, offering no threat to the Dark Angel. 'If there is a lesson to be learned, it is that all things end. And that the ambitions of mortals are nothing compared to the games of the gods.'

'Silence!' Puriel's hands rose further, knuckles whitening with the tightness of the clench. 'Do not speak your blasphemies to me.'

'Blasphemy?' Luther laughed. 'When did truth become blasphemy? If you want to learn from me, you will have to be prepared–'

'I am not a student and you are no teacher!' snapped Puriel. He took two quick paces and his fist flew, catching Luther on the cheek even as he raised his hands to defend himself. Though augmented, he was no legionary and the blow knocked him sprawling over the chair, landing hard on the stone floor. 'This is not a lesson, it is a confession, you traitorous cur!'

Luther raised tentative fingers to his face, prodding gently at his cheek. Pain shot through him, the bone fractured from the blow. He dared not get up, seeing pure hate in the gaze of his punisher. Puriel's chest heaved with deep breaths, massive shoulders flexing beneath his robe, like a bull readying to charge again.

'Only the Lion can hear my confession,' said Luther, sitting up. 'I made no oaths to you, Puriel. You have no right to stand as my judge.'

'Have I not?' The Supreme Grand Master grimaced. 'It was your command that slew thousands of my battle-brothers.'

Luther said nothing else, refusing to accept the man's accusation with a defence. Puriel regarded him with a baleful stare for some time before withdrawing to the door.

'We will get to the truth, Luther. You and I will speak again.'

Luther started to rise, but before the door closed the scene shunted again. Puriel appeared briefly at the open door, looking intent, and then vanished before reappearing inside the room once more, the door firmly shut behind him. Each shift was accompanied by a sense of decompression, the sharp pain in Luther's cheek and a hiss in his ears.

Thoroughly disorientated, he slumped down on the floor, temples throbbing.

'You testified to Master Farith that you could see the future,' said Puriel. He seemed more relaxed than before. His hair was short again, face clean-shaven. Luther started to piece together what was happening. Each jump was a time-shift of some kind.

'The future? I can barely keep my thoughts in the present…'

'So it is a falsehood.'

'I am no arbiter of truth any more,' lamented Luther. 'My mind is adrift, fractured from the flow of time it seems. There are gaps, memories, visions…'

Luther lapsed into miserable silence, feeling wretched and displaced. Only the pain of his cheek felt real: a pain that was as raw as the moment Puriel had struck him, though obviously some time had passed since the blow had landed.

He pondered this for several minutes while Puriel watched him in silence, eyes never straying from his captive.

'Time is passing for you, but not for me,' Luther whispered.

'Stasis,' replied Puriel. 'This cell is timelocked by the Watchers in the Dark. Death from old age and infirmity will not free you from your debt to us, Luther. Only when all of your followers have been caught and cleansed will we allow you to die.'

'We? For whom do you speak? The Imperium? The Emperor?'

Puriel crouched, coming down to Luther's eye level.

'You are dead to the universe, but for me and the Watchers. Like the Lion, you perished in the catastrophe that befell Caliban when traitors of Horus tried to seize our home world.'

'I was never a slave of Horus!' Luther pushed to his feet and Puriel rose with him. 'That is a lie!'

'You know all about lies, Luther of the Cursed Tongue. Your lies damned the sons of the Lion and until that deceit can be expunged, we cannot know peace. So decreed the Council of Farith after the breaking of Caliban and so shall it be for a hundred generations, if necessary.'

Luther's argument was cut off before it reached his lips, subsumed by a sudden image of thunder and fire.

A battle. A numberless horde of green-skinned creatures. Twin suns burned overhead. A river ran with blood, a bridge broken in its midst. The noise of battle and a fever heat struck Luther like a hammer, sending him reeling against the cell wall with a cry.

The vision stuttered back and forth with his immediate environs, overlapping and then replacing them, before moving further away as though falling down a hole, until Luther was alone with Puriel once again.

For a few seconds the Supreme Grand Master was a corpse in armour, glaring at Luther with dead eyes in a skull face.

'The beast…'

'What of the Beast?' demanded Puriel. 'What do you know of our war against the orks?'

Luther said nothing, unsure of anything except the sensation of reality blurring. The memory of the vision was quickly receding, but it brought to mind something far older, buried deep in his mind.

He looked at Puriel and saw something different in the Space Marine's expression. Uncertainty. Luther smiled.

'Let me tell you of beasts.'

Caliban is remembered for the forests, but it was more than simply covered with trees. Soaring mountain ranges touched the clouds, cut by deep valleys never reached by light of day. Kilometre-wide rivers twisted across the landscape like foaming serpents, sometimes narrowing to torrents so swift it would break a man's bones to dare them, other times forming lakes so vast that their opposite shores were unknown to each other.

A beautiful world. Emerald Caliban.

A planet of dangerous moods too. Storms that would swell within the mountains and tumble down to the lowlands, bringing wind and rain so ferocious they would sweep away all but the oldest trees and sturdiest walls. Spring floods swallowed whole towns. Tremors in the ground would open chasms in minutes, devouring buildings that had stood for centuries. Blizzards buried forts and their defenders.

Yes, a land that refused to be tamed by human hand.

We had tried, of course. Since the Dark Age of Technology there had been colonists. Invaders, in truth, as opposed by hostile forces as any army that had set foot in a foreign nation.

Death world they called it, but it was a planet filled with life. Just not life that would mutely submit to the rule of interlopers from another world. One could not help but love and respect Caliban, which for generations had endured our presence.

No settlement greater than a few thousands of souls could survive, save for when great Aldurukh was raised and carved from the bedrock itself. We speak of villages and towns but they were in truth keeps and fortresses. Nobody lived beyond the walls. Not for long, at least. Exile was the greatest punishment our people feared, to be cast out to the uncaring wilderness beyond the illusion of safety our walls and towers gave us.

The first defence was against the ground and the elements, as I have said. Erosion was a foe more dangerous than any other, and more highly prized than war leaders were engineers and masons. King-artisans ruled some lands, hoarding the secrets of forebears who knew of strut and buttress, guarding for themselves vaults containing the secret equations that had once guided the first machines to build walls and roofs on this world. It was the work of the ancients, archeotech. Later I would learn another name for such technology from the servants of the Emperor and the agents of the Machine-God.

Standard template construct.

The engines no longer worked nor could be found, but we had designs that had survived Old Night, and even a handful that Mars and Terra had forgotten. Pillaged now, of course, along with everything else that existed before the arcologies of the Emperor.

Briar and root and branch were the next assailants to be considered. And the course of rivers, the spread of fen and flow of underground torrents. Active, the administrators called it. An active xenography.

Of course, we know better now, do we not? Alive, alien, *guided*. It was not simply hostile evolution to blame for the adversity of Caliban, but a purpose within that sought conflict, that actively opposed our presence whilst feeding upon it. It desired to topple our towers and break our walls even as it devoured our defiance and thrived on our stubbornness. Yet it would not simply execute us, for it desired to continue the wars between humans, and twixt us and it.

We knew, of course. Not with the proof that could be laid before a tribunal, nor with a certainty that spanned every settlement. But we *knew* Caliban was alive and abhorred us. Any man or woman that had taken a turn at gate or rampart had heard the hatred in the cry of the wind. The creak of the trees conspiring, the growl of rocks grinding together as they foreshadowed our ending.

A presence, or awareness, that transcended any individual leaf or bough or brook, but was all and yet none of them.

But never was the enmity of Caliban more evident than when one looked into the eye of a Great Beast.

The forests, mountains and skies teemed with life of wing and fur and scale. As dangerous as Caliban was, it was bountiful too. Not all creatures were alike. Not every bird was equally feathered, as we used to say when I grew up. Mutation, as the Martians would call it. Corruption, others later said.

Some of the people thought these oddities were blessed, and to be revered. Some called them spirit-touched and made signs to ward off evil if they saw a six-legged mouse or caught a stormcrow flying about their tower with fanged beak. Many gave them no heed at all, just curiosities of nature that meant neither good nor ill.

The Great Beasts were both godly and terrible, reviled for the destruction they wrought and yet respected for what they were, as one learns to regard the gathering storm cloud or the telltale shiver beneath the feet. Elemental, as I said, and temperamental.

And wicked, sometimes. Not just hunters that were after prey, but determined foes that detested our presence and wished us destroyed. They possessed a strange sentience: to look into an eye of black or red or amber was to know that the thing that possessed that orb was not only of giant stature and furious strength, but also equipped with intelligence and a maliciousness to wield that wit to your poor favour.

For as much as we did not hate the Great Beasts, many of them hated us.

The vilest that ever walked the lands of the Dordred Heath, the realm of the settlement of Storrock where I grew to knighthood, was called the Horn of Ruin. Its title was a joke, of sorts, for not only did it sport a large spiralled horn above its uppermost left eye, its cry was almost alike to the deep note of a hunting horn, as though in mockery of our parties sent after it.

The Dordred Heath may have been actual heathland in centuries past, but much of the hillside had been reclaimed by the trees and brush by the time I was brought there. Certainly by the coming of the Horn of Ruin, in my twenty-first year as the Terrans would reckon it, such open space that existed in the Dordred Heath was just a few hundred paces of burnt girdle around the walls of our castle. Every autumn when the trees were starting to sleep, we sallied forth with oil and flame and scorched back the growth of spring and summer, and every autumn it seemed as though that reclaimed line approached closer and closer to the wall.

It was in late summer, as we planned the next great burning, that a ragged band of knights from neighbouring Ardford arrived at the gates beneath a banner of parley. They were in a desperate state, seven of them only, and so the ruler of Storrock, the Lord Torchwarden Neverill Bayste, ordered the gates be opened and the Ardford knights were permitted entry.

Not one of them was unmarked in armour or flesh and two did not survive the following night despite being committed to our healing halls as swift as was possible. The Lord Torchwarden bid the others to join him in his chambers and there we heard a sinister tale.

'Tell me,' said the lord, 'what brings knights of Ardford this far east of the river?'

They shuddered at the question and gave looks amongst themselves until the most senior of them, a greybeard with a scab-shut cut upon his brow and an emptied bolt-lance at his back, broke the uneasy silence.

'I am Forstor, the seneschal of the Lord Waterwatch,' he told us. 'Of the seven that you have admitted, we are the only ones left of twenty that set out to hunt a Great Beast, and it being the third party to do so perhaps the only survivors of forty-five men and women in all. We are grateful for your sanctuary, lord, and I am sure our master will make reparations for such resources as we use, but on the morrow we must return to Ardford as soon as able to bring the news of our disastrous expedition.'

'You are welcome and no cost incurred is owed by your lord, for I am sure that Marathol would honour our bonds of knighthood in similar fashion were the fortunes reversed,' said our lord, being a good man and a sturdy leader. 'And I would not have sent seven back to the woods where thirteen have perished.' The lord pointed to my gain-father next to him then, the man to whom I had been entrusted to learn the ways of knighthood. 'Aurnrod, my seneschal, will take a guard with you and see you safe back to the banks of the Briartwist river.'

'Your generosity is spoken of along the river and across the ford, and it gladdens me that the rumour is underspoken and not a boast,' said Forstor, his voice a-tremor with emotion, for it must have played hard on his mind to make the return to his home having suffered much.

'This Great Beast,' said my gain-mother, at the shoulder of my father. 'Speak of it so that we know the creature we might face.'

At this Forstor's face paled and his hand trembled about his ale mug. He finished the cup's contents and took a breath.

'I'll start at the beginning, if you might indulge,' he said, moving his mug forward a little. My mother saw the gesture and recognised the request, and so filled the ale cup again from the jug. With another draught, Forstor began.

'Ten days ago we received a crow-letter sent by Dunsany Clayd, the mistress of Fishwick half a day's travel north of Ardford. In that she told of warning she had received from the Lord Mountgard at Springwell, another day up the river. A Great Beast had made its lair at the headwaters and started preying on the fisherfolk of Springwell. Of little concern to us, you might think, but Dunsany Clayd's letter said she had received a messenger two days later, saying that the knights that had been sent to clear out the monster had been slain. Such things happen, it's true, but it was worse still. The Great Beast, riled by the attack it seems, came at Springwell itself that night. It scaled the palisade uncaring of the bullets and spears of the sentries, and broke into the homes of the Springfolk, slaughtering at will. Forty-nine died and over a hundred fled into the headlands.'

'Springwell is no more?' said our lord, saddened by this news for he had distant cousins in the headwaters settlement. 'What of those that escaped?'

'The creature went after them too,' replied one of the other Ardford knights, a young woman with blood-streaked blonde hair. 'For a day and a night and another day, taking a few each time before retreating into the woods and attacking again from another place.'

The sorry tale continued, mostly from Forstor, aided on occasion by some insight or detail provided by one of the others. For the most part we listened in silence, shocked by what unfolded.

Only two score of the villagers survived to reach Fishwick, and the following night they found the Great Beast had followed. Fishwick had an even smaller wall than Springwell and the monster threw itself at the defenders without a care, its call like the drawn-out note of a hunting horn, as I said before. Another thirty-two died before it was driven off, clawed and fanged and crushed by a great clubbing tail. Its hide was thickly scaled, decorated with tufts of thick black fur; bony brows protected its eyes and its spine was ridged with angular protrusions. It was adept at climbing, finding easy purchase with its long claws and powerful arms.

The people of Fishwick did not dare leave their homes, for such meagre shelter they gave was better than being set upon by the Horn of Ruin in the wilds. Instead they sent messengers to their neighbours for aid.

'Alas, my lord thought perhaps they exaggerated, and so despatched ten knights, armoured and well equipped,' lamented Forstor. 'When two days had passed and they had not returned, he sent fifteen more, thinking perhaps that they were waylaid at Fishwick, unable to leave the defence of the town.'

'And when no word of them arrived, you were sent with twenty,' finished my gain-father with a sad shake of the head. 'A piecemeal response, I must say.'

'But one proportionate to the need, we thought,' said one of the younger knights. 'We feared to empty our garrison and have the Horn of Ruin come upon our walls with lesser guard. We went to aid our neighbour, but the greater defence we kept for our home, which was our right.'

'Hindsight is a luxury of the living and no solace to the dead,' our lord warned, rising from his seat. 'This is graver peril than I thought and we shall muster a host that will match the threat. As Lord Torchwarden it is my sworn duty to keep the lands east of the river free, but as a neighbour and leader it is my burden to respond to those in greatest need. A hundred of my knights will ride to Fishwick and this Horn of Ruin will trouble the people of the Briartwist no more.'

As it was decided, so it was arranged. That evening my gain-father chose the ninety-nine companions that would go with him to Fishwick, myself included. It was a rare gathering, for though Storrock was home to eight thousand souls, barely three hundred were of the grade to bear arms for the lord, and our artisans were stretched to keep their armour and bolt-lances maintained. Yet the lord did not think it too many and we opened the armouries to bring out the wargear for the following day. As each gun was oiled and the batteries of our armour were installed, night was falling.

'Get a good night's sleep,' my gain-father told us, but it was not to be so.

When the last rays of the sun had touched upon the outer towers, the night watch were greeted at their posts by a terrible cry from the darkness to the west. A drawn-out note, low and haunting, like the sounding of a monstrous horn. All that had spent time in the company of the Ardford knights knew well what made such sound and the refugees themselves gave out their cries of horror.

'It has followed us!' moaned Forstor, tearing at his beard in dismay. 'I tell you it is a vindictive monster that would see dead any that have raised weapon against it.'

Forstor and the rest of the Ardford company then made a remarkable offer.

It has come for us, and us alone,' said the seneschal, to the agreement of his four saddle-kin. 'Let its wrath fall upon us alone. Open the gates and we shall sate its vengeance with our lives.'

'It was our folly that brought this beast here,' said another by the name of Ardinor. She laid a hand upon the pommel of her sword as she made an oath. 'We shall take one last opportunity to see done the deed our lord set us, and avenge those that failed in the attempt.'

'Spare yourselves,' said Forstor. 'This misery is not yours to share. Its malice is not held back by stone or exploding bolt. I beg your pardon for the error of bringing this disaster to your threshold. Perhaps the blood of those it seeks will sate its anger.'

The lord grew angry and stood before the Ardford knights as another monstrous call sounded from the distance.

'I would not buy the safety of my people with the lives of others,' he chastised them. 'What worth is a castle that offers no sanctuary? My word I have given that you are safe here and I will not break that oath even if the walls themselves should fall down this instant. I forbid you to leave the castle while this creature threatens you.'

'I will not swear an oath to it,' admitted Forstor and his companions voiced their like minds. 'If four can save the lives of scores, it is a fair price.'

They begged us to let them go forth, but the Lord Torchwarden would lend no ear to their pleas.

'You are guests here, but for your safety you shall be taken to the keep and kept within,' commanded our lord. And so it was that the visiting knights were taken back to the keep and locked in a room near the summit. Their cries carried across Storrock, pleading to be set free to end the beast's rampage with their sacrifice.

'Pay them no heed and make ready the defence,' said my gain-father.

Upon the towers we lit the great lamps, their mirror-focused beams shining out far across the scorched surrounds, to the edges of the encroaching forest. As pale yellow light danced across the boles and boughs, there came glimpses of things moving beneath the canopy, and within the canopy. A great stirring of myriad creatures rippled through the woodlands, as was sometimes witnessed in the time preceding a great quake or storm break. Not all were small things, for we spied the glinting eyes of large hunting cats and the branches shook to the swinging of carnivorous monkeys each as large as an adolescent human.

The menacing horn sounded again and the woods exploded with answering screeches and chatter. Howls and moans surrounded us, drifting across the stillness of the burn-ground, and in the cacophony it was hard to tell from where the Horn of Ruin had called. Once again the monster bellowed, longer and louder, until the trees swayed to its passage. From the north-west came the fury of trunks snapped apart and from the ruined timber strode a Great Beast the likes of which had not been seen in the Dordred Heath before.

It came as a bear on all fours, broad of haunch and shoulder when it stood upright, claws glinting like iron in the lamp-light. At first it seemed the shadows made it larger but as it approached the vastness of its bulk was revealed truly: five, six times the height of a man, and of girth to match. The tail of which we had been warned ended in a weapon like a fluted mace tipped with a spike, as big as a water barrel. Scales like tilting shields covered it.

The wall guns spoke their anger.

Trailing white fire, their shells crossed the lit sky to become blossoms of the same around the Great Beast. Seeing that horror swallowed by the bright flames made my heart soar, and others gave voice to their happiness. But their cheers were short-lived, for as the fire subsided it was clear that the Horn of Ruin was unscathed. In the dying glimmer of the strike we saw clearly its features, its lips curled back from sword-teeth, a dozen eyes arranged haphazardly around three slit-nostrils drawn open in an immense inhalation. Patches of flame clung to its hide where bristled fur had grown, but of wounds or even discomfort there was no sign.

Shaking its massive head, the Great Beast advanced, falling to all fours as it lumbered onto the scorched plain. The master of the arsenal gave voice to reload the cannons and fire again, but our lord gainsaid the command and bid the gunners to conserve their ammunition – if the fusillade had not hurt the monster in the first salvo it would not do so at the second or third attempt. They were to hold fire until point-blank range. Had we then any armour-piercing ammunition the story might have ended differently, but such were the threats of Caliban – the forest, beast and enemy knights – that airburst incendiaries were far more deadly to the bulk of foes. Its hide was better than the armour of a battle tank, its sheer bulk defence against the heat of the flames.

The squires were still roused from our preparations and were now put to work in arming the household before the Horn of Ruin reached the walls. What blade and bolt might do that the cannons could not we dared not give thought as we donned our powered plate alongside the lord himself. The hundred that had been chosen for the next day's expedition reached the walls even as the beast came close enough and the turrets roared again. This time the shells hit directly, and the howl that swept over the rampart in the wake of their booming detonations was part anger and part pain.

Though smaller in calibre than the bolters of the legionaries that later came, we had then similar weapons. Some artisans had retained the mass-reactive fuses favoured by the Imperium but our ammunition relied upon a timed trigger charge, with an impact detonation causing a secondary explosion within the target. Assuming, of course, that the shaped head of the bolt penetrated first. We knew that having shaken off the cannonade, the scaled flanks of the Great Beast would be all but impervious to our sidearms. Our range was limited by the accuracy of our weapons and our ability to pick out vulnerable target points in the face and where limbs joined torso beneath hip and shoulder.

The wall guns gave a final welcome as the Horn of Ruin came within two hundred paces, a couple of the rounds cutting deep with slashing fire, but it did not slow the monster. It broke into a run, the ground rumbling with its tread as it pounded towards the western towers and wall.

I was no legionary, nor even a soldier of the Order at that age, though I held the rank of knight in Storrock. Though I was born in Aldurukh, no man or woman ascended to the Order except by merit. Sons and daughters of the Order were sent to gain-families in other settlements having been squired until the cusp of adulthood. So I stood upon the wall of a home in which I had not been born, sworn to a lord chosen by the Grand Master of the Order to be my liege, flanked by a family that I had been given to. My fear was very real, I can tell you. The Horn of Ruin defied belief. Rising up, its forelimbs would reach the top of the curtain wall, and I could see why the lesser defences of Fishwick and the other towns had proven no obstacle.

It was my gain-mother that voiced the first concern, though prompted by duty, not dread.

'Should we not sally forth and stop it reaching our homes?' she called to our lord, recalling perhaps how the monster had laid waste to the people of the river towns without regard for whether they were soldiers or not.

I confess my first thought was the hope that the lord would not agree. As much as the walls would be little hindrance, I wanted to remain upon them rather than try to tackle the Great Beast from the ground.

'We hold here!' the Lord Torchwarden commanded us, lifting his blade and dragging it through the air as though drawing a line that the beast would not cross. 'No foe enters Storrock while we draw breath!'

We readied our arms, taking position at the rampart with elbows rested on the battlements to steady our aim. *Mouth or eyes?* I asked myself. Which would be the more vulnerable? It gave me something to think about as the hulk of scale and claw bore down upon us, a few last flames still burning upon its scaled flesh. The mouth was the larger target but the eyes had to be softer, I reasoned.

'Await the command,' the seneschal reminded us. I relaxed my finger next to the trigger and remembered to breathe, as the instructors at Aldurukh had taught me. This was not my first battle. Not even my third or fifth. I had fought Great Beasts and I had skirmished with the knights of rival lords. Even so, it was an effort to keep my grip sturdy and my aim true as that nightmare loomed larger and larger before me.

At one hundred paces distance I slipped my finger into the trigger guard again and sighted afresh, choosing the eyes. They were the softer target but it meant staring back into those raging orbs as the Horn of Ruin thundered closer and closer. It seemed as if its baleful gaze were for me alone and it came to my mind that this monster had followed the seven knights of Ardford for many kilometres, tracking them to this fortress. For what reason?

That stare bored into me, as if the creature were trying to remember everything, that it might recognise me again at some future day. There was intelligence there beyond a hound or raptor, perhaps even the sentience of humankind.

At seventy-five paces I breathed out slowly, ready for the fusillade order.

The Great Beast lumbered to a stop, claws digging furrows in the short grass that had reclaimed the scorched ground. It put back its head and let forth that disturbing cry, rearing to its hind legs once more. It thudded back to all fours and stood there, glaring from one part of the wall to the next, its gaze unmistakably moving from tower to tower and then to the gate. Finally it raised its many eyes over the wall and beyond, to the houses and workshops dug into the hillside within the ring of fortifications, then to the squat keep at the top of the mound.

'What is it doing?' I remember another knight beside me asked. Herricks her name was, and she was of a similar age to myself. I could hear the fear in her voice. I shared it. Not the violent heart-thumping moment of imminent battle that had gripped me before, but a more spine-stiffening apprehension. The dread before the terror, the apprehension of the most terrible thing that has yet to reveal itself.

'The Ardford knights,' I whispered, remembering that they were held within the keep.

And still the full dread was not ready to reveal itself, for the Horn of Ruin did the most remarkable thing: it turned its back to us and returned to the forest's edge. There we saw it at the uttermost extent of the lights, occasionally glimpsed by the guttering flames of our incendiaries, prowling in the darkness, quieter than a shade panther.

The first watch passed and the chimes rang the middle of the night and still it was there, half seen moving left and right along the periphery of the trees.

'We cannot wait all night and set out with fresh strength in the morning,' my gain-mother warned the lord, and he agreed.

'Stand down the company,' he said to the serjeants. 'Quietly, and bring up the standing watch.'

So in twos and threes we left the wall, replaced by serfs and squires with las-lances and arquebusiers. We returned to the garrison house beside the arsenal but did not divest our gear. On benches we sat, armoured for battle, but even as my chin touched my gorget in the first nods of sleep, the muffled call of the Great Beast resounded over Storrock, rousing us immediately.

As we hurried from our hall we expected to hear the crack of the cannons and see the flash of their fire, but the wall top was dim and only the last echoes of the monster's cry broke the night stillness.

'No attack,' the seneschal told us, having been on the hardwire from the armoury to the wall captain.

We groaned and swore, and I voiced the reason.

'It taunts us,' I said, astounded by the concept. 'The beast taunts us!'

And so the night passed, with an almost hourly wakening by the horn-cry of the beast in the woods, until the first touch of dawn on the canopy. With the sun's coming, the Horn of Ruin vanished, leaving only broken timber and claw marks in the fresh growth to tell of its passage.

Both weary and wary, we gathered for the expedition to Ardford, our complement increased to one hundred and twenty now that we had seen the creature we might encounter. Its size was daunting, but the greybeards smiled and claimed to have slain larger prey in distant days. Always there was a former beast more ferocious or larger or swifter or more malign.

Our large destriers were left in the stables, for the forest was at full growth and the only path they would have been able to follow was the trail of trampled foliage left by the Horn of Ruin, which we had no desire to use. Squires on more nimble mounts forayed ahead, confirming that the monster had turned south and was some distance away.

'I beg you to forget this errand,' Forstor asked of the Lord Torchwarden. ''Tis clear to us now that travel to Ardford is folly and the monster will waylay us ere we can reach its walls.'

The lord then took us aside, myself, the seneschal, my gain-mother and a few others that were counted leaders among the warrior class.

'Make all speed for Ardford,' he bid us. 'I have a fear that you will find only death there, in which case you are to return immediately. You should be able to make it back before sunfall, the day is yet long in waning and you leave early.'

'And should Ardford still stand?' asked my gain-mother. 'We defend it?'

'Its walls are not as great as Storrock's, their guns inferior to ours, I cannot imagine it will hold such a fiend at bay.' He then gave my gain-father a letter in which the Lord Torchwarden granted sanctuary to Marathol the Lord Waterwatch and all his subjects, without oath or debt. If I had wondered before, I knew at that moment why the Order had sent me to Storrock, for though it was not of great size or power in the wider region, its lord and knights were the embodiment of all that a soldier of the Order represented.

'He'll refuse,' said Tancreth, a knight older even than my gain-father and the lord. 'Ardford is one of the Old Keeps, and it's been in Marathol's family for thirty generations. You'd prise the blade from the grip of a Grand Master before getting him to leave.'

'It is only for a few days,' said our lord. 'We will combine our hosts and, our loved ones safe in Storrock, slay this Great Beast. He is prideful but not stupid.'

Tancreth and my gain-father both looked as though they would disagree, but the lord's demeanour made it clear that there would be no further discussion.

We took with us trumpeters and banners, though we did not sound the march on leaving lest it attract the attention of the Great Beast. As an army, not vagabonds, we would travel, and the squires made good time cutting passage through the new growth for the knights to follow.

We headed westward and a little north, as direct as the land allowed towards the Briartwist river. Naturally, this being Caliban, the river's course was not a certain thing, the land about it prone to shifting as much as anywhere else. Settlements like Ardford and Fishwick were built upon the hardest, tallest hills near the banks and from season to season might have a gushing torrent at the foot of their walls or a five-kilometre walk to their fishing boats.

As the sun passed noon, we had the knights from Ardford attend to us in the vanguard, they having most recently passed this area. While they had done so in hasty flight, they recalled enough of their route that by the lead of a few landmarks – particularly large or otherwise notable trees, rocky slopes and mounts impervious to the movements around them – they could guide us with some accuracy, though the sky was hidden for kilometres at a time by the high canopy.

An off-worlder might think that the Great Beast would have left some trail in its pursuit, as it had done in its withdrawal the night before. An off-worlder would not understand that the most menacing of the Great Beasts were not simply large creatures, or even malignly intelligent predators, but of a nature wholly attuned to the environs of Caliban. Their presence stirred the surroundings, sometimes elevating the aggression of nearby predators, often animating the liveliness of the flora. Trails were wont to disappear within days if not hours, even of the heftiest creator.

Our squires and the Ardford knights were no strangers to the woods, however. As summer waned to autumn there could be seen the subtle distinction between the freshest growth and the darkening leaves and stems of the plants older by even a few days.

So it was that before early afternoon we descended into the Briartwist river valley, making good time.

We had pickets out, of course, to keep watch for the Horn of Ruin. Not only behind, but ahead. We thought the creature more than capable of assuming our intent and moving before us to waylay the expedition before it reached Ardford. In fact, the closer we came to the town the more convinced I became that we would find the Great Beast there, squatting in the rubble as it patiently awaited our arrival. I shared this misgiving with nobody, for I did not want my companions to think me a coward or hysterical.

The ground about the Briartwist was fenland, empty of all trees but for a scattering of copses, cut by ancient causeways made of stone that neither frost nor quake could wear down. On leaving the woodland we sent the squires further ahead with scopes and they returned swiftly with the news that Ardford remained, the walls intact, smoke rising from its houses and forges.

With these glad tidings to lighten the mood, knowing that no return would be made that day, we relented in our haste and took our care to pass the marshes without incident. It was still some time before dusk when we came within sight of the citadel beyond the ribbon of the Briartwist and all that remained was to negotiate the river itself.

Though the ground on the western side of the river was solid enough, the fens were not suitable for any foundations and so no permanent bridge could be erected. The old causeways met each other about a kilometre and a half upstream, but the movements of the river meant that for most of the year that junction was quite often some distance from the flow, or beneath it. Still, it was the safest place to navigate available – hence the position of Ardford to guard this crossing. Pontoon bridges provided a more temporary measure when the waters were wide and slow, but the knights of Ardford informed us that such crossings were destroyed as part of the defence of the town, to give the foe no easy passage.

Still suspecting to have the Horn of Ruin at our backs at any time, we went northwards and found that the ford was quite navigable, the river bending through a broad stretch where the causeways met, the footing secure enough.

It was almost anticlimactic when we came to the crossing. We had reached Ardford unmolested, not a sign of the Great Beast for the whole journey.

And then the sky resounded with an ominous hunting cry behind us.

I cannot say why the Horn of Ruin chose then to attack. Was it a tactic to trap us against the water, or just happenstance that it came upon us as the squires set foot into the low river? Had it waited until we were within reach of our destination, granting an illusion of sanctuary that heightened its own excitement? Perhaps it even chose that moment to tempt reinforcements from the township, forcing those within to decide whether to remain behind their defences or sally forth in assistance.

It also presented a dilemma to my gain-father. The Great Beast was still some way behind us and Ardford little more than a kilometre and a half distant.

'The lord will welcome you into the walls,' promised Forstor, pointing across the waters to the smudge of grey on the nearby mount. 'We can make the gates before this fiend catches us.'

'I would not bring this foe to the door of my neighbour,' argued the seneschal. 'A terrible choice we would force upon Marathol.'

'I would not open a gate with such a monster close at hand,' said Tancreth.

'And should it come upon us in line of march we will be

ill-formed to meet its attack,' added my gain-mother. 'Better to make preparation and gather our strength.'

'You are fools,' the leader of the Ardford knights shouted, wading into the ford. His knights followed and several of our company made after them, thinking to restrain them.

'Let them be,' commanded the seneschal. 'Maybe they will bring aid. Either way, we cannot count their arms to our credit. Form up for the battle, we shall hold the far side of the river.'

'Why such cowardice now? Last night they offered up their lives to save us all,' I wondered aloud.

'I think their offer to give themselves to the beast was a ruse,' declared Tancreth, spitting as he watched the other knights leave. 'An excuse to get outside the walls and flee, more like.'

As we followed our lord's order I briefly longed to be back at the wall of Storrock, a feeling that intensified as the Great Beast approached, ploughing through the marshland towards us. Fen that would have sunk an armoured knight to the waist was no obstacle to its powerful legs, though thick mud splashed its dark scales and weed tangled about its limbs like nets.

'Fire by volley, on my command alone,' my gain-father told us, holding his bolt-lance at the ready.

A passing thought made me check the batteries of my armour, for I was tired from lack of sleep and the march and wondered how drained was my plate. The reserves were good, fifty per cent and more. Likewise, the squires had brought ammunition by the score, to supplement our own packs, so there would be no cause to relent except death.

The closer the Horn of Ruin came, the larger it seemed, silhouetted against a darkening sky. Yet the new perspective also brought some hope, for I realised that being on the rampart had us at a level with its head, and so an ideal height for attacking. We were as vermin to it, and if we moved smartly enough perhaps its bulk would be its disadvantage.

I clung to such hopes for the minutes it took for the Great Beast to plunge through the marshlands, choosing to ignore the voice in my head that told me the dead knights of the other settlements would have thought the same.

'Ranging shot… Fire!'

I pulled the trigger of my bolt-lance and the explosive projectile leapt from my weapon, streaking some one hundred and fifty metres to hit the chest of the creature. Too low. The propellant we used then was far less efficient than that of the Legions, but easy to manufacture. The Horn of Ruin was at range, albeit our volley did nothing to impede its advance, and it did not even greet the salvo with a roar or groan.

At one hundred paces we were more sure of our mark and the command came to fire three rounds. I pulled my trigger thrice, aiming higher than before. Sharp metal clattered from its monstrous features, exploding moments later with little effect, but a few detonations seemed to break open scales or darken an eye. I had no idea which had been mine amid the welter of gunshots.

This enraged the Great Beast and it crashed forward now, fountains of mud and water erupting from the fens, a spume of white like a ferry's bow wave when it hit the river proper.

'Free fire,' my gain-father commanded and we needed no further encouragement.

As a massive wave splashed across the ford, droplets filling the air, we opened fire as quickly as we could. This was not a test of marksmanship but discipline, as when in wars of old great blocks of soldiers would exchange volleys until the resolve of one or the other failed.

Ten rounds fired in as many seconds, I swapped the magazine of my bolt-lance and fired again, emptying the second in similar fashion. A gunline of a hundred and twenty knights is no small thing, even for a creature the size of a keephouse.

I don't doubt that much of our fire went astray or expended harmlessly upon its thick scales, but its thrashing through the water became more desperate as it neared the bank upon which we were arrayed.

The water foamed dark with blood in its wake.

On reaching more solid ground it seemed to find fresh vigour, baring its fangs even as bolts exploded over lips and tongue.

Water streaming from its claws, the Great Beast bounded out of the river and across the wet ground between it and the first line, faster than anything that large should move. Three knights perished instantly, pierced or crushed beneath its feet. So determined were the nearby warriors to fire that they held their ground even as the massive jaws snapped down, sweeping up four more.

Body parts joined the stream of blood that flowed from its jaws, which yawned wide again, spilling corpses. A huge foot rose and this time the closest knights evaded, breaking to the left and right to avoid its crushing descent.

I was in the second line, firing over their heads. I saw pieces of my fellow knights wedged between cracked teeth and it sickened me. To this day I swear I saw Erl Irsak still alive though bit in twain, his face a mask of terror and pain as he flailed between two teeth like monoliths. For years after I would wake in a sweat with the memory haunting my dreams.

The front line broke formation with the beast in their midst, lessening our fire considerably. Some dashed beneath its bulk, firing into its underside with little visible effect. It turned, tail swinging with ponderous but terrible grace, smashing aside a handful of men and women, throwing them hard against the blood-puddled dirt of the bank.

I regret that I became so possessed of my duty to continue firing that I took little notice of what else occurred, and to this day remember only the clamour of shouts and screams, the deafening bellows of our foe and the thunderous reports of our weapons. Perhaps the oversight most grievous was that I did not see my gain-father fall. Others later told me he attempted to hurl a handful of grenades into the maw of the enemy, but in doing so was swept into its jaws. The explosives detonated, causing great harm to the beast, but slew him also if he was not already dead on the monster's fangs. I fully believe that he knew what would happen and chose the act of sacrifice, for that was the measure of him in every experience I had.

Battle is often brief but harsh, or elongated and tension-filled, but the fight with the Horn of Ruin was one of the most intense yet drawn-out affairs I remember. I recall having to exchange my weapon with that of a fallen companion because the breech was too hot and threatened a misfire that would have torn off my arm – as happened to one of the other knights just moments later.

Victory was hard-won, right unto its final moments. Along with a score of others, as the creature faltered I charged. I took my blade two-handed and hacked without much skill, arms working more by boon of my powered armour than the weary muscle within. Its face a bloodied mess, blood pouring in a river from its wounds, when the beast finally died it buried two more of my keep-kin beneath its collapsing bulk and its death-animated tail smashed aside another.

Forty-one warriors of Storrock gave their lives that day while the knights of Ardford looked on from their walls.

'Not a pint of blood thicker than cat's piss between them all,' Tancreth declared, now commander of our troop. There was certainly no evidence of the bravery Forstor had so vocally announced the night before, and it seemed Tancreth had reasoned rightly their cause for wishing to quit the defences before the Great Beast had arrived.

We gathered the dead and wounded, and though messengers

swiftly arrived from the nearby township none of us was of a mind to spend that night amid strangers. I and no few others were also vehemently opposed to coming into the presence of Forstor and his knights, for the laws of hospitality would surely have been broken if I had come face to face with a man that had abandoned my gain-father before his final battle. That they had brought this doom to our walls and we had not returned the ill-favour was high in my thoughts for several days after.

The whole matter soured relations between Storrock and the river keeps, fomenting a border skirmish that had not been resolved before the coming of the Lion and the ascendancy of the Order years later.

We returned with heavy hearts to our homes, but found the walls well-guarded and those within safe, and judged the sacrifice to have been necessary. We mourned the lost, tended the injured and hailed the feats of those that deserved it.

Two days after our return, squires came back from a patrol to the south. A Great Beast had been sighted in the Wellvale, a day's journey from our halls. As swiftly as that, the Horn of Ruin, our worst foe and largest of the Great Beasts ever to plague the Dordred Heath, became history.

Puriel regarded Luther for some time, brow knotted.

'I ask of orks and you speak of forest beasts,' he said eventually, shaking his head. 'If I thought you might be of aid, I was mistaken. You do nothing to level the debt you owe the Lion and his sons, but spin tales of your own past glories.'

'If that is what you take from the story, then I can do no more for you. I could speak more plainly, but would knowing your doom help you avoid it or bring it about? I am no seer of talent, I dabbled in the foresight but swiftly learned that it is a road that leads to more peril than answers.'

'Do not speak so freely of such sinful sorceries!' Puriel raised a fist and Luther drew back, fearing a blow. The legionary held his clenched hand for several seconds and then let it fall to his side, eyes narrowing.

'You speak of foresight and in your story your leader died fighting the Great Beast. Is this a warning? Or guidance… Your gain-father succeeded even in death. Am I to perish while breaking the last of the Beast's strength?'

'The warning is in the whole story, not the parts.' Luther sighed and turned his head away. 'What happens to you is unimportant. There is always another beast.'

Puriel snorted and footsteps receded, followed by the slam of the door. Luther felt the momentary tingle he now knew preceded the stasis of the Watchers.

TALE OF THE LION

Whether by the sorcerous curse of the storm or the temporal manipulations of the Watchers, Luther's perception became increasingly detached from the linear flow of time. What was memory blurred with what was to come and what was happening, at times so fractured that he went insane, losing even himself amid the riotous flurry of images and recollections. He saw Puriel again several times, and others came to him with threats and admonishments. Always it was one, the Supreme Grand Master, accompanied only by the Watchers and no other Space Marine. He was, it seemed, held in secret even from the rest of the Dark Angels.

Others sought insight into the whereabouts of his followers and through fleetingly lucid encounters, Luther pieced together some idea of what might have happened, though he also learned that at least two thousand years had passed since Caliban had died and a warp storm had engulfed his host. His people had been scattered, it seemed, all but for Luther.

Two thousand years was a long time and even though he did not truly know how long a Space Marine could live, he found it hard to believe that any Calibanites could have survived so long. Yet the questioners kept coming, demanding to know of this individual or that, reading from a growing list of names. Some he recognised, many he did not, and he was forced to remind his captors that the Order had numbered tens of thousands of knights when the Lion had returned.

Most of his interrogators left in anger, but no few encounters ended in pain, either inflicted by his visitor or through the mental torture of his temporal dislocation. It was not rare for the questions put to him to trigger visions and memories at the same time, and the intervening periods of stasis only served to further his uncoupling from the natural course of events. He remembered fighting in battles that had not yet taken place, and seeing the faces of warriors not yet born as they died beside him. He visited planets whose names he did not know, or lifted blade against aliens the like of which he had never seen in real life. Nightmare, prophecy and recollection became inseparable.

Then came a period when he was visited by a lord of the Dark Angels called Morderan, who kept him free of stasis for some time. The act was not out of any compassion but a desire to centre Luther's thoughts on current events.

'I am something of a student of yours, you could say,' Morderan told him during his fourth visit.

Luther had been washed, the wound on his cheek dressed by Morderan himself, who had also delivered fresh clothes. After many days, twenty or thirty perhaps, Luther's ravings had subsided and though he still suffered flashes of nauseating othersight, sometimes he went for hours without experiencing any kind of warp hallucination.

'My predecessors and I have been thorough in the taking of notes, even when you have been at your most incoherent,' explained Morderan while Luther finished a bowl of tasteless protein gruel. 'I have read them many times, trying to glean some substance, a single thread, from your disparate meanderings.'

'I am at a loss to aid you,' Luther confessed. 'The tether of my mind to one time is thin and swiftly broken. I do not choose what I see, and cannot choose to unsee what has been presented.'

'I fear there is something else that guides your visions, and not to the good purpose of my Chapter,' Morderan replied. 'Sometimes we must risk drinking from the chalice even though we suspect it to be poisoned, lest we die of thirst anyway.'

'Is that what I am? A poisoned chalice!'

'Certainly.' Morderan scratched a brow scarred and creased. 'One from which I must drink again, it seems. Tell me of Cypher.'

'You mean the Lord Cypher?'

'I do.'

'You need to be more specific. I say this not only for your sake, but for mine. If I delve into the past too broadly I fear I will go astray again, and that does neither of us any good.'

'Cypher was one of your closest advisors.'

'The Lord Cypher was a ceremonial role for much of its history, dating back to the earliest days of the Order. But the Lord Cypher in the latter days of my command was an important member of my retinue. There was little of my design that I did not confide in him, and he was chief among my advisors on all matters of the arcane. But you know this if you have read my previous utterances.'

'When did you last see him?'

'During the defence of Caliban, but you should know that even before my tribulations in prophecy my memories of that time were unreliable. The storm, you see. Even as it stole parts of my mind, it scrambled what had happened. These days you have granted me have been little use, I am sorry to say. I can place many events, but out of sequence and some may be entirely fictitious, products of imagination.'

'He survived the fighting, yes?'

'I have no idea. I don't recall seeing him die, but that does not mean it did not happen. I have a recollection, vaguely, of hearing that he had been cornered by Corswain. If true, it seems unlikely he left the encounter if Corswain survived.'

An odd look passed across Morderan's features, which Luther could not wholly decipher. It seemed connected to the mention of Corswain rather than Lord Cypher, but Luther had no chance to pursue the matter before the Dark Angel spoke again.

'You recall my predecessor, Alloken? He died fighting orks recently.'

'I have decided it is better not to enquire after faces no longer seen. It only leads to more confusion, and often anger against me.'

'A stranger clad in the livery of the old Legion seemed to intervene on behalf of my brothers, aiding us against the orks. It is not the first time we have encountered him, wielding bolt pistol and plasma pistol. My research leads me to believe that this individual may be Cypher, but I do not know why he would help us.'

'I assume that you did not treat him as friend on previous occasions?'

'There are times he has been seen assisting our foes, that much I have as fact. I think he knows more about the Fallen and the storm that took them than you do.'

'Fallen?'

'Your followers. The traitors saved from retribution by the powers of the warp. They have fallen from the light of the Emperor.'

Luther suppressed a laugh, knowing it would invite physical censure. It astounded him to hear a Space Marine speak of the Emperor in such terms, as though He was almost… divine?

'If it is indeed Lord Cypher that you seek, then tread carefully. Not all hunts end with a kill.'

I was twenty-six years old when I returned to the Order. The encounter with the Horn of Ruin and other quests had established me as a courageous warrior and a capable leader in the eyes of the Lord Torchwarden. Along with seven others I was despatched to Aldurukh to face the decision of the Grand Master. Would he readmit me to the ranks of the Angelicasta or send me back to Storrock? My friends were likewise eager to impress, for it brought honour to their families to be accepted into the Order.

To understand why the Order was so special, it is important to remember that neighbours were as likely to war with each other as form alliances, and both in the turning of a few years as circumstance changed. Caliban was unforgiving and although some preached the code of tolerance and cooperation, since the terrors of Old Night and the resurgence of the planet's biosphere, nothing like any central or even regional authority survived. The lands within sight of the peak of Aldurukh were considered the domain of the Order, under its protection, but it was no nation, the Grand Master was no king. Some rulers, like the Lord Torchwarden and the lords of the riverbanks, were bound by ancient familial and civil oaths to respect the boundary of Aldurukh and offer mutual assistance should it ever be threatened by foe of bestial or human origin. The Order itself remained apart from the politics of the settlements, and to towns further afield was regarded almost as myth.

Yet the Order was the bastion of strength around which human life on Caliban revolved, whether they knew it or not. It accepted only volunteers, not heirs, as my own young adulthood demonstrated. Skill at arms was tested, but all that were accepted began training anew as if born as squires or serfs until they exceeded the requirements of their tutors. Temperament was equally examined. The Order was founded upon merit, a last bastion of ideals that had been swallowed by Old Night. Its knights were expected to be true to their word, to uphold the honour of Aldurukh, to forsake all titles and inheritances of the outside, and to dedicate their lives to the improvement of oneself through martial prowess and the protection of others.

Human nature cannot be wholly ignored, and there were knights of the Order who were brash or ambitious, sometimes vain or aloof. Yet in spite of their personal weaknesses they placed fraternity above all else and strove to overcome their worst qualities. There was no concept of perfection, no thought of pinnacle, as embodied by the spiral, which can get ever tighter no matter how far one travels. To progress, to show willingness to learn and to serve was as important as sword arm and bolt pistol aim.

I am pleased to say that all eight of us passed the scrutiny, bringing with us testimony of our peers and lords that shone light on our deeds, while mock battle proved skill at arms. Lord Cypher scrutinised the soul, as he did until the end, and found the best knights of Storrock were fit to the purpose of the Order.

In leaving Storrock we had renounced all other oaths, being released from bondage to our former lords as preparation for our admission. If we had failed, we would have been too shamed to return, becoming freelances and the Wandered. Instead we pledged allegiance to Aldurukh and its folk, and on naked blade shed our blood to the brothers and sisters of that place, and in kneeling before the Grand Master submitted to his authority alone.

I was reunited with my mother and father, now as equals rather than parents and child, for it was possible that I might one day be their superior. The Order was a family of a different kind of love, surpassing the bonds of blood that happened to exist between us.

It was not long before I regained my rank of serjeant, for I had not forgotten the lessons of my youth. As such I was second-in-command of the patrol to which I was assigned. All about the mountain the forests were divided into wards, to each assigned a squadron of ten knights. A small enough force to move at will and pose no threat to local lords, but potent enough to handle all but the fiercest Great Beasts. And should such a threat arise, the Order was not slow in sending reinforcements nor calling on the lieges of the lands they helped keep safe. We were kept separate from the lands where we had been raised, in my case being assigned to the squadron that patrolled north of Aldurukh, far from Dordred Heath.

The following winter was harsh, with blizzards faster and longer than many a scarred serjeant had seen, and certainly the worst of my young life. For days at a time the patrols were unable to leave Aldurukh or forced to seek shelter in the homes of the local rulers. After weeks of incessant snow some passes and valleys were entirely closed to us, and the Grand Master, at that time a venerable commander called Tomsas Karrad, feared for the settlements that lay beyond. He initiated a plan of clearance expeditions to open up the worst-afflicted areas, sending out hundred-strong work teams with axe and shovel to clear what they could.

It is a sorrow that the Great Beasts were not so waylaid by the snows as our knights, and many strange and dangerous creatures were drawn down from the high peaks and the northern glaciers by the brief ice age. Great Beasts were not the only threat, for natural predators like mountain wolves and timber lions were starved of prey, and driven by hunger they ranged further and further afield, into the domains of the lords.

The clearances were perilous enough, the elements and terrain accounting for several dozen of our people in the first days until we honed our practices. Ice crevasses swallowed some, others were caught in avalanches, while at least a score were picked off by hungry animals when they had become separated from their companions. Progress was slow but steady, and still the dark storms showed no sign of relenting. On the fourteenth day since the clearances had started, a team reached the far end of a canyon known as the Shouldersplit Pass. As might be guessed by the name, some ancient upheaval of the rocks, or perhaps the artifice of our forebears, had split a mountain almost in half, so that a great ridge rose on either side of the valley. Generations of melt flow and spring rain had softened the valley floor and it caught the sun until past noon – when sun could be seen, of course, which it hadn't for nearly the whole winter. Significantly for me, Shouldersplit Pass was within the ward that was allocated to my squadron. It came to us to protect the workers as they continued. So we rode forth from Aldurukh with that objective.

The forests were almost unrecognisable, boughs heavy with white, many trees splintered under the weight of their snowy burden. Beneath the canopy the going was easier, only knee-deep for a knight and of no hardship for our destriers.

Let me tell you now a little more about our mounts, for one might not understand what magnificent creatures they were, and it is a lament of mine that their breeding was forgotten after the coming of the Imperium. Told to me by my birth-father, as he had learned from generations before, the destriers had been created from the finest equine genetic stock during the Dark Age, before such resources were lost during Old Night. Large and swift, these animals were bred also for their intelligence and, so the legends claimed, the grandsires of the destriers that we rode had once been grafted with devices that even made them capable of speech. We no longer had the means for such communication, but to the last of them the destriers remained capable of high empathy with their riders and I would happily swear they understood all that we spoke to them even if they were physically unable to reply.

Not only intellect but other features were enhanced far beyond natural evolution. Stamina and strength, enough to carry an armoured knight for many days with only a few hours' sleep each night. And by armoured I mean the battery-powered warsuits I and my companions of the Order wore, not simple metal plate. The greatest of them could bend steel with a kick and easily snap bone with flailing hooves. They were loyal, bonding with a rider for life, and tales abounded of mounts that had fought to the death to defend a fallen knight, and of destriers that would not return to their homes when their rider was lost but disappeared into the woods seeking their mistress or master.

I had three destriers over the course of my life, each as dear to me as a family member. Dearer, in fact, for as I have said the bonds of family were considered less strong than those of mutual service. The first, Accadis, which means Blackfire, was given to me before I left for Storrock and she came back with me to Aldurukh. She it was that bore me that first winter, a brave and inquisitive soul that knew well her rider was of rank and destiny, and hence prone to bouts of imperious behaviour towards her fellow destriers.

Another remarkable ability of the destriers was their tracking sense. Not for us the need for packs of hunting dogs to catch the scent of our prey. Our steeds could follow a days-old trail as well as any bloodhound.

So it was that when we were four days out from Aldurukh protecting the latest extension of the clearance to the north, Accadis pricked her ears and whinnied meaningfully to me. The squadron had split, with Serjeant Gabrio, my senior, leading five knights west of the route of advance while we covered the approaches to the east. We had not seen the sky for a day, having entered the lowlands and forests proper just after dawn the previous day. The snow was thick, drifting still from the branches above, so that it was dark as night but for the glimmer from our saddle lights that reflected on snow and ice.

'Patrol halt!' I called to my companions, my hand moving to the bolt pistol holstered next to the saddle bow.

They responded without comment, falling silent as they reined in their destriers. The quietness brought the distant calls of the work groups nearly two kilometres behind us, but save for that the only sound was the creaking of trunks in the wind and the odd thump as a branch's load proved too much.

The other destriers caught the scent too, exhaling sharply, stomping warnings with their forehooves. The wind was in the south-east, behind us and from the right.

'That's towards the diggers,' exclaimed Parican, turning in the saddle to look back along the trail we had forged in the snow.

'Something circled around us?' suggested Larel, pulling free her pistol.

'Or coming down the east shoulder,' I replied.

Accadis was fretful, drawing attention to her unease as a warning. I could feel her pulling at the reins, straining to take us towards the scent.

'Bear arms,' I told the others, taking out my pistol. 'Corboric, take lead. Take us back east of the work group. We'll put ourselves between them and whatever is coming.'

We fell in behind the knight I'd commanded, riding single file at an angle away from the route we had taken. This was an old stretch of forest, the trees like castle towers in girth. Even atop Accadis the plume of my helm did not touch the lowest branches and had I stood on her back I would not have been plucked from my perch.

We rode as straight as could be reckoned through the broad trunks, the slope of the land rising to our left, becoming steeper after a kilometre. The snowdrifts worsened, thick against roots coiled like mythical serpents, and our steeds were slow in picking their way forward in places.

Their agitation grew as the morning wore on. We had no chronometer – Serjeant Gabrio had the squadron's only timepiece – but by the vaguest notion of the sun's position I reckoned we were coming close to midday when ahead there erupted an awful shrieking of birds and monstrous bellows.

It is hard to gauge distances in the press of the forest but the thrashing of wings through the leaves could not have been more than three or four boltfalls ahead – a boltfall being the typical distance a bolt's propellant could last before it started to lose horizontal distance, so in total five hundred to eight hundred metres. As the disturbance passed, the unseen flock flying almost due north which put our prey south of us, we moved on cautiously. Here and there an older tree upon the slope had lost the battle against the white of snow and tumbled, leaving breaks for the twilight to creep in. We quickly extinguished our lamps because they showed our position far more than they illuminated anything of the creature we hunted. We could not see much more than half a boltfall ahead and our ears were more guide than our eyes, even though the boles of the trees were thinner and more separated.

It was then that the snorts of our mounts alerted us to patches of darkness in the snow and a few metres later we came upon large furrows where something had passed, accompanied by glistening droplets. Blood. It was difficult to judge direction of travel in the gloom but the destriers kept pulling southwards and so we let them take us onwards, easily following the tracks.

Soon we saw something in the distance, a bulk of darkness beneath the shade, unmoving.

I signalled for the others to spread out, leaving Egalade a

short distance behind us to watch the rear. We pulled free our chainswords then, charged from the small generator packs carried upon our steeds. We saw more clearly what was humped over a fallen trunk ahead. Where the tree had collapsed, the canopy was broken, letting in fitful pale light.

It was a Great Beast, furred with white and dark grey, the hairs as long as a destrier's mane. Though it did not move, we approached warily in case it was simply playing dead. We could not see its head, but spines like sword blades jutted from its shoulders and rump. It was easily three or four times larger than one of our steeds and an outflung paw was as big as my body, tipped with seven claws that could rake out the guts of a knight with a single blow. A gasp from Larel, who was approaching ahead and to my right, caused us all to flinch, and the cause of her reaction became clear as we rounded the beast, still a good score of metres distant from the creature.

The pale fur around the throat and chest was matted with glistening red. The flesh was shredded, skin lying in flaps, and one side of the monster's face was sunken, as though it had been staved in by a smith's hammer or equally powerful blow.

'Serjeant!' Parican's call was more hiss than whisper, his eyes wide as he pointed to the ground beside his steed.

Another furrow in the snow led away from the steaming corpse, heading westwards. Spatters of dark red followed the line. The blood of the beast. It was difficult to say what had left the tracks but it was smaller than the dead creature, and within a dozen metres they suddenly disappeared.

'Where do they go?' demanded Larel, but a careful search of the surroundings revealed nothing else on the ground.

I returned to the spot where the tracks ceased and looked up. The branches above were clear of snow.

'It went up,' I told the other knights, pointing with my sword. 'Disturbed by our approach I reckon.'

'Must have been a really nasty monkey,' said Larel, her jest breaking the tension that had been building, drawing laughs from me and Parican.

'The apes have all migrated south,' said Corboric, unamused as he looked back at the savaged monster. 'A cat? Lion perhaps?'

Before we speculated any more, the stillness was broken by the bark of a bolt pistol firing, six shots in all. It came from the direction of Egalade, three score metres back. As we turned towards him his destrier started whinnying and stamping something fierce, the rider clinging on barely with his sword hand, bolt pistol held aloft.

'I saw something!' the knight shouted to us, but the rearing of his steed made it impossible for him to show us where.

Accadis reacted before me, leading her stable-kin as she burst into a gallop, first running for her distressed companion before veering south again, nostrils flaring. I pulled on the reins, slowing her a little, but allowed her to show the way. We plunged into darkness once more and I lit my saddle lamps. Peering ahead, I saw something moving fast through the limits of their beams, passing behind the trees a boltfall or more away.

'Catch it before it gets into the trees again!' called Corboric, his mount dashing past us on the left. The others were drawing level on the right, separated by a score of metres. I glanced back and saw that Egalade had joined the rear of the chase. Together the squadron thundered between the trees, coming upon scuffed tracks in the snowdrifts. Passing one bole I spied bright red splashed up the trunk. To my mind it looked oddly like a handprint and I thought again of perhaps some carnivorous gorilla forced to hunt large prey by the terrible winter. The recollection of the Great Beast with its throat ripped asunder made me shudder.

'It's wounded,' I called out, and at the same time I signalled for Corboric and Larel to move aside and ahead so that we would encircle the creature, as we had done at the clearing.

Close to a kilometre the pursuit continued and I marvelled at the speed of our prey, but stooping from my saddle I could see that it was flagging, the tracks becoming shorter, more laboured.

'We have it!' announced Larel, about a dozen metres further ahead.

A tree as broad as a roundhouse dominated the forest before us, its vast canopy overshadowing everything so that for perhaps a hundred metres nothing else broke the white of the snow, drifts falling in the wind as the branches swayed overhead. The two lead knights converged from left and right towards the base of the trunk, where I spied something pale against the bark. My first impression was a mane of long, yellow hair and I thought again of a lion, though the creature seemed more upright than any feline. I saw claws, long and bloodied.

The others closed with pistols raised and ready, their chainswords growling. The creature snarled in reply.

And in doing so the hair fell back from its face and I looked upon the visage of a man. Eyes the colour of Caliban's forests regarded me from amid a grime-covered countenance, alert and full of intelligence.

'Hold!' I cried, sharper and swifter than any command I had given before.

I could scarce believe what I witnessed and dismounted to see better. As far as I could judge, the person was a little taller than myself, but other than the outstanding blond mane was bereft of hair, like an adolescent. I could tell, for he was fully naked, body as dirty as his face, the splash of fresh blood down his chest and along his arms from hands to elbows.

Swallowing hard, I remembered that this person – if it was indeed a person – had attacked and slain the Great Beast we had found. It seemed impossible.

'It is one of the nephilla!' warned Corboric.

'Nephilla do not bleed,' I told them, for I could see that the youth's shoulder was a bloody mess, the flesh exposed down to bright white bone. 'Your panicked volley found its mark, Sar Egalade.'

'I did not panic! A bolt hit would have torn off a man's arm,' the knight replied, keeping his eyes fixed on the apparition backed against the tree bole. 'It is not human!'

The green eyes slid from me to regard the others, narrowing as they moved from one knight to the next. I could see calculation in that gaze, one that I came to know very well in the years after. He was weighing up strategies, visualising what would happen.

'You saw what it did to the quest beast,' said Larel. 'Keep clear and fill it with bolts.'

'You're not going to attack, are you, Lion?' I said loudly. I am not sure why I gave him the name; it was a poor joke to settle my nerves. To find a person when we had been seeking a beast was most unsettling, and as you can imagine I had no idea of the manner of person I had discovered.

I laid down my pistol and chainsword and took a step forward. The youth tensed, but whether to attack or flee I did not know. Pain flared across his face as he moved his wounded arm. I fixed my eye upon his and slowly advanced, hands held out with the palms down. I could feel the aim of my companions sighted upon the boy but I trusted them not to shoot without my command. I hoped the youth made no movement though. In their state, my knights surely would have thought it an attack on me and opened fire. A very different future for Caliban and the Imperium had that happened.

As it was, I came within arm's reach and leaned forward, brushing aside the hair so that the others could see what I could.

'Look,' I told them. 'He is a man, not a beast.'

And that was how I found one of the Emperor's primarchs.

As he had done several times before, Morderan stared hard at Luther as though he might extract what he wanted to know by simple visual study. Luther knew well the use of the pregnant pause in conversation and interrogation, leaving a heavy gap for other participants to fill. He was not sure if Morderan thought he would volunteer more information, or the Dark Angel simply needed this long to think. Either way, Luther kept his silence until Morderan spoke again.

'You liken Cypher to the Lion,' he said quietly.

'I liken the encounters to one another,' Luther corrected. 'At the time of my meeting, I knew nothing about the Lion or what he would become.'

'And you think we should deal with Lord Cypher in the same fashion? To treat him as an ally?'

'As a man. I know nothing of his intentions, nor his loyalties. Neither will you if you slay him out of hand.'

Morderan's eyes widened, first in shock and then revelation. He stared again at Luther and stood up, more animated than he had appeared before.

'Cypher was one of the most influential members of your cabal. Certainly your warriors owed allegiance to him. If there is one that could command them, it would be him.'

'Or Astelan, or Griffayn, or Maegon.'

It did not appear as though Morderan had heard Luther. He paced back and forth, talking to himself.

'He might be the key to the whole conspiracy. If we capture him he could lead us to many others, hundreds or thousands perhaps.'

The Supreme Grand Master started towards the door, quite forgetting the other man in the room. Luther stood, feeling that the intent of his story had been missed entirely.

'I might have been wrong,' he called out. 'There are many that think I should h-'

TALE OF THE BOOK

'–ave let him be shot.'

Luther fell silent, as though suffering a verbal stumble. Morderan was at the door, his expression grave. He had a pistol in his hand, the first time Luther had seen the Space Marine bearing any armament. Morderan's lips were moving silently, his posture swaying back and forth as though he debated himself.

Luther's eye was drawn again to the bolt pistol. It was finely crafted, its main block inlaid with pieces of green and black stone to fashion the symbol of the Dark Angels. He could smell the fresh lubricant and Morderan was also heavy with the scent of cleansing.

'Have you a question?' Luther said quietly, not liking what he saw but not wishing to watch matters simply unfold without his participation.

Morderan glared at him, the pistol half rising.

'It was you that told me to capture him,' growled the legionary. He thrust an accusing finger at Luther. 'You! Make him an ally, you told me.'

A wave of grief passed over the Supreme Grand Master's face and he faltered, his hand falling back to his side. Luther judged it to be just half a dozen metres between him and the Space Marine. If he was quick enough…

He still would not be strong enough. Not to wrest a weapon from the fingers of a fully transformed Space Marine. And such action would certainly precipitate violent reaction. Probably lethal. When pressed, a legionary's first reaction is to slay, not injure.

Luther was tempted all the same, not for want of freedom but desire for release. The relative stability he had enjoyed in the captivity of Morderan had revealed to him the depths to which he had sunk in his prior madness. Those depths awaited him still. Even the dislocation of this latest stasis leap was starting to eat at the edge of his thoughts.

How much time had passed? Years, obviously. Decades? Likely.

At least three thousand years had passed since Caliban had died and yet Luther had known perhaps forty days of it with any semblance of clarity. Many more were the days spent raving and raging, locked in loops of prescience or chained to the wall while a screaming face demanded repentance he could offer to nobody but the Lion.

He realised his thoughts were already distant, a living dream, when he felt the cold muzzle of the bolt pistol pressed against his cheek.

'You are a poison,' snarled Morderan.

'You may be right,' Luther replied as he closed his eyes.

He waited, breathing slowly. The pressure of the gun made his face ache, but he welcomed the sensation, anchoring him in the present. If he was going to die, he wanted to be there, not abroad in some hallucination or vision.

'Your lies nearly destroyed us.'

Luther wanted to deny the accusation, but stopped, sensing that it might be the last provocation Morderan needed. At the last, it seemed Luther was not yet ready to die. Not without meeting the man he had betrayed, to explain why he had turned and how he now regretted it.

He opened his eyes and looked sidelong at the Supreme Grand Master. The gleam in the man's eye spoke of a mania Luther had never seen in a Space Marine. They were supposed to be conditioned against such mental breaks, recruited from the strongest-willed so that they could face any adversity.

But he could see in the face of Morderan that the fear was not outside but within. The enemy he faced was himself, whether real or perceived. What had he done? They had last spoken of Lord Cypher. Morderan spoke of alliance. Had he somehow parleyed with the foe he had been chasing? Bargained with him?

Morderan focused on Luther, saw his gaze meeting his own. He stepped back, the muzzle of the bolt pistol wavering in his grip.

'Your lies end here!'

Luther flinched but the bark of the bolt pistol rang around the room for a moment before the heavy thump of Morderan's body hitting the floor. He stared down at the corpse, stunned, seeing the bloody mess where the head had been seconds earlier.

His eye slid to the bolt pistol still in the grip of the Space Marine's right hand, the smoke of its use drifting from the barrel, and then to movement in the shadows at the door. He stooped to grab the weapon as red eyes gleamed.

His fingers passed through thin air.

The following moments passed like staccato visions, a stuttering series of frozen images that snapped the last bonds to any sense of the present. Adrift, Luther fell into memory and vision again, unable to settle himself within his own lifetime even as he knew his thoughts flew astray.

He shouted and spat, hurled abuse at his captors and swore every oath and curse he knew against the Watchers in the Dark. He threatened and cajoled, begged and sobbed, demanding the Lion hear his testimony so that he could be released from this misery.

In all-too-brief moments of clarity he looked upon his wretched existence and wept.

'The punishment has outstripped the crime!' he wailed, falling to his knees before the latest grim figure to confront him.

This one seemed young in comparison to the others. Unlikely that he had risen to his position without great effort and age, but his looks had a boyish quality that set him apart from those that had come before. Perhaps it was this peculiarity that allowed Luther to focus a little.

'Do you suffer?' the Space Marine asked, bending one leg to kneel next to Luther where he was sprawled upon the floor. 'Do you understand the pain you endure?'

'I know it,' Luther croaked back.

'Good.' The Space Marine stood. 'It is but a fraction of the torment you deserve.'

'The Lion...'

'Take his name from your tongue lest I cut it out!'

Luther fell silent, broken.

'I am Zapherael. I need to know about Praxas.'

'What of it? An unremarkable world.'

'You visited it.'

'Once, to take the fealty oath of its ruling council. It was a supply world for Zaramund, and when we took the port planet they were content to continue their previous relationship.'

'You mean when Zaramund was taken by the Fallen?'

'The Order.' Luther pushed himself to a seated position and looked up at the Space Marine. 'This is not about Praxas or Zaramund. It is about my followers.'

Zapherael's scowl was answer enough.

'I have been in this cell for...'

He looked at the Space Marine to finish for him.

'Five millennia and more,' Zapherael said.

'Five...?' Luther almost choked on the word, shaking his head. He covered his eyes for a moment, rubbing the heels of his hands hard into his face to bring some kind of sensation. 'Five thousand years have passed since I last spoke to any soul outside of these walls. You must know more of what happened to the Order than I can ever say.'

'To know our enemy we must understand their trajectory. If I can know their history I can predict their future.'

Luther uncovered his face and pushed himself to his feet. He nodded, lips pursed.

'A laudable notion, but be wary of how far down that road you travel.'

Even the straightest-looking road can sometimes lead you astray, and most that are worth following are far from straight. Even at the journey's end it is easy to look back upon all the winding turns, hills and dips, and see an inevitable line from the start point to the present. We become blind to all of the junctions, forks and opportunities to leave the road altogether. Thus we remove ourselves from the blame of becoming lost because we set out with good intentions.

On Caliban we had a saying about good intentions: *You cannot steer the arrow once it leaves the bow.*

When the Lion called for a war against the Great Beasts it seemed like the most glorious endeavour we could undertake. The Order, all of humanity on Caliban, was arranged by that age-old conflict. Rid of the predations of these creatures, we would gain even greater glories.

Except none of us stopped to think what would happen

after the beasts were dead. Well, perhaps the Lion did, but he never shared his thoughts. We assumed that with the land rid of its most horrific monsters we would live in peace with our neighbours.

We were wrong.

Even when the crusade was declared there were dissenters. The Order was not the only force of note on Caliban, though it had swelled to become the largest and most powerful. Others thought that the Lion planned to use the pogrom to take control of their castles, to occupy lands for the benefit of the Order. I cannot place my hand on my heart and swear they were wrong, though it never entered my mind to speak against my gain-brother.

Most of our opponents were swayed by my diplomacy, and outright bribery on occasion. I learned much statecraft in those years, even as the Lion honed his strategic prowess.

Some held out and later relented, but there was one organisation that would never find alliance with us. They were the Knights of Lupus, and they argued that the Lion demanded fealty not allegiance, and swore they would never give it to a lord of the Order.

So we crushed them.

I could regale you with tales of that war, but it is not a period I look back on with any joy or triumph. Many a knight of the Order lost their life fighting fellow Calibanites, when before the Order had stood aloof from such conflict. Was it necessary? Probably. Was it desirable? Perhaps not. Like a Great Beast, we cornered Lord Sartana and forced him to fight. I would have done the same as he, I think, now that I have looked upon the Lion's works from a different perspective.

But even though Sartana was likely justified in his defiance, he was not right. The Knights of Lupus were, by the definitions of our later settlers, corrupted. I understand so much more now than I did then, of what the Knights of Lupus had done to survive, and how it had come to pass that they had made pact with the intemperate spirit of Caliban. They knew better than we did the nature of the world and the role of the Great Beasts.

Even so, they were mistaken in thinking they could control that spirit, as many others have been before and since. I cannot point the finger at them in accusation without first acknowledging my own blindness in this regard.

When we confronted them at their fortress, we discovered that they had been capturing the Great Beasts and turning them into creatures of war. As I regard it now, it was a masterful strategy, to turn enemy into ally, or at least servant. Yet the Great Beasts were tainted as was the heart of Caliban, and so all that treated with them were tainted by extension. This much was not so obvious at the time, but failure to confront the quest beasts seemed justification enough to eradicate the Knights of Lupus. It certainly served well the Lion's choice to eliminate their resistance. I could not admit to myself then what I later thought, but it was in this battle that were shown the first signs of the Lion's ambition.

It pains me to think about such matters. Every argument I voiced to support my bid for independence comes back to me even as I think of how we argued to exterminate the Great Beasts. Though the truth was ever a flexible tool in the later years of the reclamation of Caliban, I would say that I never lied. Never wholly.

But this story is not about the Lion, it is about how we follow the road and take one turn or another, but can never really say whether we will reach the destination for which we set out. Certainly when we destroyed the Knights of Lupus there was never any thought that we had sown the seeds of our own destruction, the end of the Order.

Dramatic? I think not. Though it is always possible to trace cause and effect back through distant history and say that if only this had happened or that had not occurred things would have been better, I say with all earnestness that the war against the Knights of Lupus was the turning point in the history of Caliban, the Order and the Dark Angels. Had we found peace with them, had they submitted or even had I not stepped into their fortress, I may have trodden a very different path.

Is it self-centred to claim for myself the blame for the destruction of an entire civilisation? Of course, but it is also not wrong. For in the household of Lord Sartana I came upon his library. As I have said before, knowledge from the Dark Age and Old Night was scarce and scattered, so I cannot be faulted for wishing to investigate this trove of books. But even as I looked at the first tomes I knew that this was something that was not meant to be known. And at the same time it awakened in me a desire to understand.

We should have burned the library and all the corrupting works within, but I did not command it. Maybe the books themselves sensed their impending destruction and reached out to me. I cannot say it would be the oddest encounter I have shared with them.

I did something that should not have been done and, by direct consequence of that decision, I sit here now and my world is destroyed, my oaths broken with my legacy one of misery and treachery.

I took the books.

It seemed a sensible enough act at the time. What did it matter if I preserved a few pages of old lore? It was easy to come to quick justification, as everyone does who knows deep down they ought not to be doing what they are. They could contain knowledge about the Great Beasts and aid in their hunting… What ancient designs or intelligence might I glean from the pages? Might I find a means by which we could tame the forests themselves?

All the reasons come freely to mind but the one that has condemned more of us than any other, asked rhetorically rather than sensibly: what harm could it do?

What harm?

Most importantly, it was the first lie I told to the Lion. My first subterfuge. We took the library's contents back to Aldurukh and found that most of it was of inconsequential merit – valuable but unremarkable. It was an impressive collection but replicated much of that which was in the archives of the Angelicasta – especially given that many knightly organisations had freely donated or shared their lore with the Order to cement their alliance in previous years. Some of the books the Lion and I agreed were disturbing, and I gave him my promise that they would be destroyed. He trusted me, of course, and never again inquired after those illicit volumes.

I did not think about them for some time. The campaign against the Great Beasts took us all over Caliban, far from Aldurukh and my secret library. At first the deception nagged at me. I was sure that my absence meant the books would be discovered and I wrestled with my own conscience, first devising an excuse to return to the Angelicasta but then dismissing it. The volumes were well hidden and I was a Grand Master, and hence beyond suspicion.

The longer I was away, the less I thought about it. I had almost entirely forgotten their existence by the time we finished the campaign. We know what happened next – the arrival of the First Legion and the Emperor. It was a time of upheaval and revelation, and my understanding of the universe expanded in ways I could not have imagined. With the coming of the Imperium, a handful of old books of Calibanite folk tales seemed quaint in comparison. Stories for children.

Yet still I had no compulsion to reveal their existence or make good on my promise to destroy them. Through all of the tumult of Caliban's compliance and the absorption of the Order into the Dark Angels I kept them hidden away. I cannot think what I told myself, if I needed to tell myself anything at all. Mementos of old Caliban. Trivia. Curiosities.

We joined the Great Crusade, and took part in the compliance at Sarosh. It was there that perhaps the small splinter of betrayal pushed a little deeper. It was not the books that caused the wound that widened between us, it was the secret of their keeping.

Obviously I knew nothing of that at the time. Sarosh simply brought to a head many frustrations and disappointments that had been building since the Imperium had claimed both my world and my gain-brother. The Lion was never the same after he discovered his true nature. The forests had made him a beast. We had turned him into a lord of knights. Both were guises for something far different to anything we could have imagined.

To this day, I do not know how the Lion learned of my moment of weakness. Somehow he heard that I had knowledge of the Saroshi assassination attempt. Zahariel was the only other that knew, I think, though one can never rule out the Watchers in the Dark. They see everything but tell little enough.

Banished back to Caliban for an instant of indecision, I was angry and hurt by my gain-brother's dismissal. My hesitation had condemned me as untrustworthy, even though he cloaked my imprisonment in a veil of trusted duty. No surprise is it, that on my return my resentment drove me to embrace that which I had denied myself for so long? I had been dutiful and yet a single doubt, a human heartbeat of something less than utter dedication, had seen me tossed aside.

But I make weak excuse, because I regurgitate the falsehoods I used to persuade myself that I was in the right and the Lion was in the wrong. How dare he? How dare this Emperor's son dismiss me because I almost allowed him to be killed?

Churlish is an understatement, but such was my mindset at the time, and so with spiteful intent I fell into the trap of the books willingly, as though an infant embraced to the bosom of my mother.

I can remember entering the vault where the remains of the Library of Lupus were kept, for the greater part of the books were indeed harmless and provided good cover for those that were less so. By hidden way I passed through the outer library to the small chamber within that I had concealed, with none of the precautions I took to contain the power of my later collection. I am surprised that no other soul had been drawn to the volumes, for their influence can be strong, but I assumed that the library was disused for the better part of a generation. When the Emperor takes over your world, few people think about a musty old collection of books.

I imagine it, with my theatrical recollection, but it seems to me now that there was an aura in the vault. My own excitement and apprehension I suspect. I would say that I heard the whispers of forbidden knowledge, but that did not come until much later. For all that they were the slope down which I tumbled into ruination, the volumes kept by the Knights of Lupus were merely introductory and of little puissance compared to the likes of those supplied to me by my later allies.

Forgive my jumbled narrative, it is a symptom of my time-fractured existence. Even as I tell this story I picture the events within it simultaneously, and it is so hard to separate the start from the end, the setting out from the destination. I relive even as I relate.

I could barely remember what the books contained, but was fixed upon the simple fact that the Lion had desired that they did not exist and so in reading them I defied his will. Petulant behaviour for a Grand Master of the Order, but such was my motivation.

I should say that I opened the lock with trembling hands and reverently pulled forth the first book, but I cannot. I had no inkling of the import of that moment and flung open the chest with casual disregard. I rifled through the books within and a few scrolls, then picked one at random. As random as such choices can be, given all that I have said about the nature of these particular texts. Maybe one picked me.

It was bound in board and vellum, much scuffed, the corner of the pages browned by the thumbs of many previous readers, the gilded writing nothing more than an incomprehensible lightness on the dark cover. I did not even open it at the first page but let it flop open to somewhere near the middle. I was immediately confronted with a depiction of what I first took to be a Great Beast. Fangs and horns, great shags of fur and serrated talons. Yet this apparition bore an axe in one hand and a whip in the other, like no Great Beast of the forest.

Intrigued, I started to decipher the antiquated text.

I was fortunate that no other came upon me, for I must have sat for several hours poring over that single annotated page. Most of that time I did not spend in reading the words, though they were old indeed and awkward even for one of my education and study. It was the meaning of the words that entranced me, sending me on a mental journey by their implication as I wrestled with the import of what they meant.

It would take me years – decades – before I even started to piece it all into genuine knowledge, but that first glimpse of an entire universe that I had never even thought possible left me shaking. I would not tie together the threads of Caliban, the Great Beasts and the warp until later, after much more study, but I think I must have had some indistinct sense of it even then.

My other overwhelming feeling was guilt.

I was not supposed to see such writings. I was reminded of

why it was forbidden, when the Lion and I had first flicked through the pages and seen rites and symbols that made us uncomfortable.

I resented my guilt even as it manifested. Why should I not know these things? What right had the Lion to deny me the fullest understanding of our place in the universe? I conveniently forgot my own misgivings and agreement with the Lion's ban, excusing myself because I had not complied with the demand to destroy the books. Circular logic of the worst kind, but we cast such loops about ourselves when we wish to do that which we know to be wrong.

I could read no further that day and frankly was frightened by what I had seen. Not by the monstrous greater servant of the powers, but by the image in my head of a world without boundaries, formed of our nightmares and dreams. I was afraid, intrigued, wracked with nerves and yet excited by what I had discovered.

I made a resolution to keep the books hidden from all. Not out of coveting the knowledge for myself, but for fear that others might more quickly understand their content and usurp me with that power. I was also aware that the Lion could return to Caliban and any flagrant abuses against his command would not end well for me. In taking the books I had disagreed with him as a peer, but now I was the subordinate of a primarch of the Emperor's Legions.

I became so disturbed by the notion of discovery that I soon after removed the books from the chamber in the main library, and brought them to my quarters. Although they had been concealed, I found it inconvenient to venture too often to a wing of the Angelicasta that was hardly visited at all by my companions. My journeys to the library had gone unremarked thus far, but it was only a matter of time before someone enquired as to my purpose and I preferred not to have to outright lie to my peers.

In those early years, I dabbled. It was almost pleasurable to deny myself the indulgence of study, and sometimes months would pass without me even looking at the volumes in my office. I would leaf through a tome on occasion, flipping the pages idly while I paced and thought on other matters. By keeping my arrangements casual, I fooled myself into thinking that I remained free of any real insubordination. After all, my duties of Grand Master were little enough to fill my time and I expected the return of the expeditionary fleets to end the tedium at some point.

A hobby, perhaps. A little dalliance with obscure texts that raised interesting philosophical questions. Nothing more.

The years passed and the Lion did not return. We turned the sons of Caliban into Space Marines and sent them into the void like packaged goods. Returning ships told us that the Great Crusade went well. Thousands of worlds had been made compliant like Caliban.

My idle hobby took up more of my time and I started to believe that the Lion would never return. Caliban's purpose was served well enough in his absence. Our blood continued to fuel the Dark Angels Legion. Even then I was not so discontent. I think I would have taken it more harshly had the Lion been more present. Continual scrutiny would have been an insult. I started to believe that maybe he did trust me, that his words of duty had not cloaked a hidden admonition.

I was a fool.

All doubt was erased at Zaramund.

Some worlds are carved upon history with thick strokes, while others barely merit a footnote. Zaramund should have been the latter. It was strategically well placed, a staging point from Terra for the Great Crusade, overseeing a stable warp channel that saw thousands of ships launched towards the galactic north. Years before, the First had departed Zaramund before they discovered Caliban.

I do not know why some of the populace of Zaramund rebelled. I can guess, and from experience my guesses would not be too far from the truth I would wager. The Imperium finds purposes for things and then sets them to that task in exclusion to all else. I think it is a manifestation of the Emperor's thinking, to see all else as tools. Witness Caliban! Cleansed of the Great Beasts, the forests were tamed for the most part. Beautiful and verdant. The Emerald World. All of it was torn down, replaced by arcologies to house workers and tithe collectors for the administrators of Terra. Our bountiful forests were of no use to the war effort. Weapons, armour, people. These were the things devoured by the Great Crusade and so Caliban was reshaped to provide.

Zaramund was a shipyard, but ships need crews and Zaramund was compelled to provide. Generation after generation either labouring to create the warships of the Emperor or indentured to leave upon them. That contempt for the history and people of Zaramund would breed the kind of rebellion we saw. Not a treachery from the ruling classes but a sudden swelling insurrection across every factory, orbital and far-flung station. A mood that was suddenly set alight.

And snuffed out by Horus.

The details do not matter to this tale, except that in needing a swift response to the loss of the system, Horus called upon Caliban to aid the counter-attack. I agreed and led a force of Dark Angels to the campaign, and although it was perilous and saw many good companions slain, it was also heartening to once again take up arms and be at the forefront of glorious battle.

I was never the equal of the Lion with blade or strategy, but I still rose to Grand Master of the Order. I was no neophyte commander!

And then, even as I received plaudits from the man who would become Warmaster, the Lion took it all from me. And not in private, but before Horus and the other leaders. Dismissed like the lowliest serf, an errant child sent to his chamber to think on what he had done. My fleet confiscated as though the ships were toys I had misused.

After my humiliation, before I set foot on the transport that would take me back to Caliban, two others sought me out to commiserate my unfortunate castigation. They found me in the antechamber of a launch bay of the *Vengeful Spirit*, Calas Typhon of the Death Guard and Erebus of the Word Bearers. They were divested of their armour now, but still larger than I was in my modified plate.

Typhon wore heavy leggings and surcoat, his thickly muscled arms knotted with scars of both surgery and battle. Erebus was slighter, for a Space Marine, and wore a dark-red robe, plain but for a Legion symbol. He was an imposing figure all the same, his face and head covered in tattooed symbols from chin to nape.

I had only met both a few hours earlier, at the very celebration that had led to my censure, but Typhon I had known by dint of fighting beside, or rather behind, his formidable forces in the recapture of many orbital stations and the first landings on Zaramund itself. Erebus was more of an enigma, his Legion strangers to the Dark Angels as far as I knew, his position within the Luna Wolves something of an anomaly.

'I bring bottled sympathy,' declared Typhon, offering a large carafe and three glasses. His smile faded. 'Few felt any jubilation after the Lion's intervention and it seemed a waste to let these libations be returned to the stores unopened.'

The chamber was not big, and felt smaller with the two giant warriors beside me. But we were aboard a battle-barge and the furnishings included those fit for legionaries as well as smaller individuals like myself. Erebus sat on my left, Calas on my right, each filling a chair that would be a throne in any other setting.

I did not feel much like drinking, but thought it rude to refuse the officer of the Death Guard. He poured glassfuls of dark-red wine and handed them to us before raising his own in toast.

'Brothers before sons,' he said, somewhat cryptically, though I recalled his words immediately following the Lion's edict against me: *There are those of us that know what it is like to feel the displeasure of our primarch.*

'I am not good company at present,' I told them, taking a sip from the glass before placing it on the table between us. 'Thank you for your solidarity but it is cold comfort.'

'Comfort?' Erebus raised an eyebrow, distorting the runes across his forehead. He looked at Typhon and directed his next words to the Death Guard. 'You told me Luther of Caliban was a staunch lord, worthy of our intervention. He speaks of comfort as though we should pat him on the back and tell him everything will be all right.'

'What do you mean?' I demanded, my anger flushing quickly, my patience already worn thin by weathering the Lion's accusations against me. 'I ask nothing of the Word Bearers, nor the Death Guard.'

'Be at ease,' Calas assured me. He took a large mouthful of wine, savouring it before swallowing with a satisfied nod. 'Good stuff. We have this organ, I'm sure you know, called the neuro-glottis? Enhances the sense of taste. I could track you like a hound just by sampling the air. It makes me really appreciate the nuances of a very good wine.'

I was taken aback, and starting to be suspicious of their company.

'Do you not have more important duties to attend in the wake of victory?' I asked.

'You have been robbed of the glory that should be yours,' said Erebus. He downed his wine in one long draught and stroked the stem of the glass with his massive fingers. His voice was soft but rich, and brought to mind the Lord Torchwarden, reminding me of the man I had been many, many years before.

'We wanted you to know that others see you. Your acts are not extinguished by the disapproval of the Lion. Your deeds should be rewarded.'

'I feel like I am being recruited,' I replied, taking up my glass again. Even though I was aware of the flattery being aimed at me, it was gratifying that they thought I was worthy of such attention, even as I was immune to its effects.

'I told you he was a sharp thinker,' said Calas, smiling. 'Open-minded too, I'm sure.'

I wondered what this could mean, but before I had to ask, Erebus produced a slim volume from within his robe. I recognised the design on its cover immediately, an octagonal symbol overlaid with a circle and arrows, which had featured in one of the books I had taken from the library of the Knights of Lupus.

'What is that? Where did you get it?' I asked, even as I reached out to take the proffered book. 'Is this a tract on the warp?'

Erebus looked surprised and I heard Calas laugh at his expression.

'You have seen this before?' demanded the Word Bearer, eyes moving from me to Calas.

'Caliban has its lore too,' I said as I opened the book and started flipping from one page to another, reading snippets of the small type within. There were no symbols, no diagrams or illustrations of fantastical beasts. Just words. Words that ensnared me just as much as anything I had looked at in my personal collection.

'This explains it all?' I whispered as I looked at Erebus with shock and wonder. This time it was the Word Bearer's turn to laugh.

'All? Nothing can explain all!' He placed a hand on the book, covering it entirely. 'But this is the start of understanding. It is… a guidebook? A primer. A source of answers but more questions.'

'The right sort of questions,' said Calas, leaning closer so that I could feel the heat of his bulk next to me. 'Questions like,

"Who is the Emperor?" and "What are the primarchs?" Questions you may have asked or may not.'

Indeed such questions had come to mind as I perused my esoteric library. One cannot stand in the presence of demigods and not wonder how they came to be. Not unless you have been mentally conditioned not to ask such questions. As one of the augmented, rather than a legionary, I had not been subjected to most of the inculcation therapy that had replaced their old identities with unswerving loyalty to the Legion.

Maybe I should have been.

My suspicion returned with greater vigour and I closed the book sharply.

'If I accept this, I am in your debt,' I said to Erebus. 'Your thrall, so to speak. I cannot commend you on your subtlety, for you have shown little. You see me reeling from the chastisement of the Lion and think me weak, a slower herd member on which to pounce. You are mistaken.'

Yet despite my words, I recall now that I made no attempt to return the book to the Word Bearer. He looked at me thoughtfully and shrugged.

'You see both the truth and a lie,' he replied. 'It is not weakness we see in you, but strength. No other would have stood before a primarch and suffered such indignity without crumbling. And if you find our approach unsubtle it is because we lack time, and we do you the service of believing you open to straight approach. But you are entirely correct that we would have you as an ally where currently we have none. You are important to us.'

'The book is our offering,' said Calas. 'The first plank of a bridge to build between us. To help you understand why we would want you among our brotherhood. And the wine was offered in genuine commiseration.'

'You will find a couple of other select volumes stowed with your belongings,' added Erebus. 'More specific texts.'

'Who wrote this?' I asked, turning the thin book back and forth in my hand. 'Whose words are these?'

'Mine,' said Erebus, 'but they are an abbreviation of a far longer, worthier book. A book penned by no other than Lorgar, the Word and the Mace.'

'A primarch wrote this?' I felt as if the floor shifted beneath me, as it had done when I had first examined the Lupus library. A world-changing fact. 'You mean Lorgar of the Seventeenth?'

'Yes. He is a visionary, Luther. Who else would better see the inside of the universe than one who was crafted to conquer it.'

'But…' It was hard to reconcile the thought of forbidden powers, strange warp creatures and the supernal with the Emperor-worshipping lord of the Word Bearers. Even on Caliban we had heard tell of how the XVII Legion raised great monuments to the Emperor on every world they took.

'Everything is interconnected,' said Calas, standing up. He linked his meaty fingers together, forming a single fist between them. 'Our world, the realm you know, and the warp. The powers, the Emperor, the primarchs. Even Caliban.'

'And Fenris, Olympia and every other world where a primarch fell,' Erebus added with a sly smile. 'Each resonant with a different kind of energy. They called to them, of course.'

'To know the empyrean is to know ourselves,' continued Calas. 'If we cannot understand hope and despair, strength and weakness, how are we to know anything mortal?'

Such words were honey to me, sweet and enticing. As they had been chosen to be, I realise now. A different kind of flattery, but much more than that. Calas had not been wrong when he said he knew how I felt, the abandonment that ate my soul from the inside. Few have stood at the right hand of a demigod and then been cast aside.

Here was a promise in plain words that the first book had offered silently. Vague but powerful, the offer of knowledge that would explain what had happened, how I had toppled from the heights to the depths.

And the means to right that wrong. A ladder to climb back to the summit. A tool. A weapon. All of these things and more.

All in a book no thicker than the swordplay manuals I had learned from as a youth.

The occasion reminded me of the earlier incident at Sarosh. A time of decision that would profoundly affect the way I viewed the world. Were you to offer me the ability to go back and change one decision, whether at Sarosh or aboard the *Vengeful Spirit*, I cannot say which was wrong, if either. Just like the moment in the forest, when the course of the universe hinged on the actions of one man, I was presented with a chance to see the fork in the path.

One led to reconciliation with the Lion. I would make public this conspiracy and use Calas and Erebus as bargaining chips to regain his favour. As clear as the Highmere from which Aldurukh drew its water, I saw that these two were but the tip of something vaster. I was reminded of the brotherhood to which Abaddon had tried to introduce me, and wondered at the extent of the erosion within the Legions. And Lorgar? Did this malice run as far as one of the Legion commanders?

The book I held was all the proof needed that something was awry in the Great Crusade.

Yet if I confessed to its possession and offered myself to the mercy of the Lion, what judgement could I expect? To tell of this book was to speak of the others I held, for a confession needed to be full or kept silent. I would tell him of the grudge I harboured, but back then I could not admit that his punishment had been warranted – I had weighed his life against my own ambition, a terrible crime on reflection.

I looked at Erebus, and saw that the Word Bearer had been studying me intently. His gaze flicked from me to Calas for just a split second. His expression was impassive enough, a study in neutrality, but in that single glance I read a whole script, for I am not a dull-witted man.

Calas had vouched for me, that much had already been made clear. He had some rank in this secretive arrangement, aside from his position as a senior officer of the Death Guard. But Erebus, this Chaplain from another Legion, was certainly the more powerful of the two in the room. The apex, perhaps? Or did he answer to Lorgar?

Such recruitment was fraught with risk. I knew from my own paranoia about the books of the Lupus library that an ill-considered decision or moment of laxity always threatened to leave one vulnerable. Had the Lion not arrived, perhaps their overtures would have been more subtle and extended, as Erebus claimed. Instead, opportunity had arisen to strike fast while my humiliation was still hot within me. But that opportunity would swiftly pass upon my return to Caliban.

Calas had vouched for me and Erebus was gambling on my participation.

If they had any doubts about me, any hint that I would reveal their plotting to a higher power, my life was over. Even I, Grand Master of the Order of Caliban, second-in-command of the First Legion, the Dark Angels, was not above their retaliation. Nothing but absolute assurance that I was aligned to their cause would stop me from having an unfortunate incident very shortly after our meeting.

I recalled again the bomb I had discovered at Sarosh. Would there be something other than books waiting for me among my belongings on the way to the transport? Something less culturally explosive but certainly more so in chemical terms.

As I explain it here, it may seem that I sat in quiet consideration of my fate, weighing up these facts and conclusions. The opposite is true. That glance from Erebus triggered a flash of insight and only later did I decipher my own reasoning.

Damned if I do. Dead if I do not.

Given the course of events that followed, it is no surprise that I chose damnation over destruction, and I did it willingly. Though I assessed my life chances as precarious, I had committed myself to this course before Calas or Erebus had first approached me, when I had taken the books from Wolfgard.

'It seems you are the allies I have long been seeking,' I told them.

I then quickly confided in them the extent of my prior knowledge and my possession of the books that would see me condemned. Their recognition of my sincerity was swift, for I spoke the truth and they could see it. I tell you that there is no machine or psyker as swift as a Space Marine at discerning a spoken falsehood, for he can hear your hearts beat faster and taste the fear in you. They were made to be superlative warriors but are also amazing interrogators.

We parted with kind words and half-promises of future cooperation, but all three of us knew that with my fleet taken from me my imprisonment on Caliban would be complete. There would be means to leave physically, of course, but the act of doing so would be in open defiance of the primarch's will – a will he had made known in front of everyone, from Horus to the attending army troopers.

'We shall hear if you should call,' said Calas. He extended a hand and I gripped it, shaking it slowly. 'You are alone no longer.'

'With alliance comes reciprocation,' Erebus told me, his gaze intent. 'When the time comes, Caliban will also answer.'

'If it is in my power, it shall be so,' I swore, and meant every word of it.

And that was the last time I saw Erebus of the Word Bearers.

It was more than forty years before my path crossed that of Calas. Four decades during which I expected the return of the

Lion, but he never came. Half the lifetime of a normal mortal spent in banishment on my own world, and the canker of my punishment gnawed at me every day.

A lot happened, far too much to tell all of it here. Each day widened the division between me and my gain-brother. My own plans evolved and yet never came to fruition. I had thought perhaps the conspiracy of Erebus and the others had been unmasked, their treachery expunged from the Legions.

Thirty years after Zaramund, I learned that Horus had turned on the Emperor. That was when I knew that Erebus and the powers he served had not been idle for so long.

I also had spent my time deepening my knowledge and power, but I had held back from the final commitment, never quite certain if my transgression would be uncovered. I also confess a certain reluctance to step so far over the line. Among the books that had been gifted me by the Chaplain were two that delved into the nature of the warp and its relationship to our world. Framed by his annotated text and with the aid of the Lupus volumes, I pieced together certain sorcerous rituals.

Not until I heard of Horus' fall and the massacre at Isstvan did I conclude that the time had come to solidify my new allegiance. I felt certain that the forces of the Warmaster would come to Caliban within weeks, months perhaps, and wanted to be ready not only with troops but also something deeper. I shared this with no other, not even Zahariel or Astelan, for I was not sure they would continue in their support for me if they understood that I was engaging more archaic powers to our aid.

As seems necessary, it was midnight on the longest night of Caliban when I began the ritual. I had assembled the accoutrements required, piece by piece so as not to arouse suspicion. Some I had crafted for myself. Aldurukh had grown greatly following the rise of the Lion and myself, and greater still following compliance, but was now a half-empty shell of its former glories. Whole wings and towers had been abandoned, stables and mews boarded up. The oldest chambers, those that had been carved from the mountain bedrock at the heart of the Angelicasta, had been the first to fall into disuse. Crafthouses that had not heard the ring of hammer for two generations gave me the perfect venue for my endeavours, where the armourers, silversmiths and candlemakers had once laboured.

I had not yet fashioned my secure library, but I moved my quarters to a suite more spacious and extensive so that I could use one of the chambers for keeping my growing collection. It also happened that this older tower gave passage by secret means to my crucibles and smithy.

I set all out in accordance with the diagrams I had painstakingly drawn into the margins and binding leaves of my books, for I dared not commit my thoughts to paper that might somehow be parted from me. With fingers stained by red ink as I prepared the summoning, I used salt and calf fat to draw out the octagon and the symbols around its circumference, anointing each cardinal point with a droplet of my own life fluid.

As I did so, I spoke the words assembled stanza by stanza from across five different volumes. Here the Lupus books had been most useful, for one had contained a translator of sorts, a lexicon of intonation that matched many of the archaic terms with ancient Calibanite pronunciations. As a student of lore I had already learned the older tongue, but had not realised it shared many similarities to the language of sorcery.

Candles I lit and placed in lead sticks, the wax bound in nets I had intricately woven myself from hairlike threads of silver. Other preparations were more mundane but no less secure – the locking of the doors and the heavy drapes across the windows.

I did not know what to expect. My mind drifted back to tales from the Wandered – dispossessed knights and adventurers, vagabonds that moved from settlement to settlement offering a sword arm or tongue, whichever provided best payment. Witches and quest beasts in caves, and brave knights that rode out to them. But also stories of the nephilla, and the wicked conjurers that called them to curse the heroes of the tales.

The greatest of the storytellers would throw spark powder into the firepit and dazzle us with the flashes of colour while the sorcerers chanted their vile spells.

It did not occur to me that I had become the evil wizard, or was aspiring to. I was still the lord slighted by a rival from a foreign power, struggling for freedom against an overbearing king. Usurped, such protagonists are invariably sent into the wilderness, either to die by beast or elements, or by the hand of the king's henchmen. In either style, the heroine or hero escapes their execution and returns with allies to overthrow the usurpers.

Caught between the fever of excitement and the sickness of apprehension, I began.

I had hardened myself to the very high probability of failure. Until my encounter with Calas and Erebus, a small part of me had harboured the suspicion that the works from the Lupus library were pure fabrication. They certainly contained erudite passages, but the drawings of vast crumbling manses and ravening dog-lizards had at times seemed more the product of a febrile imagination than scholarly pursuit. At my lowest moments, my confidence drained by the interminable nature of my exile, I sometimes toyed with the idea of hurling those books into the furnace, condemning them to the flames as fanciful tales of fiction.

I had not succumbed, but the probability of tapping into the nephillic powers on my first attempt, through means jury-rigged together from disparate sources, seemed remote. I placed the bar of success low, hoping to receive some sign, just a flicker or ambience that showed the slightest thinning of the veil between our realm and the world of the nephilla.

So I chanted and paced, walking the circuit as I scattered bone ash as offering into the octogram, one eye on the conjuration I had written, the other searching the symbols, the candles, the air itself for the smallest notion of the otherworldly.

With a crack like lightning the ashes took fire, the scattered flakes lighting again as though returning to the flame that had consumed them. They whirled in a wind I could not feel outside of the octogrammatic wards, spinning faster and faster until they formed a shape. A humanoid shape, the tip of the head about level with my waist. Two embers became the spark of eyes.

It had worked!

In my shock and joy, I stopped the incantation, thinking it complete. I had, after all, summoned a nephilla into the octogram. By any measure, even if it dissipated immediately, it was an unalloyed victory.

What I had not realised was that the last stanzas of my verse were the binding spell. Having brought forth the creature, my lapse into silence meant that I failed to contain it to my will…

This thing of fire stood for some time in the daubed symbols, glaring at me with furrowed flame for a brow. Then it smiled and reached out a fire-tipped finger, as though prodding at the air. It advanced a step, finger still extended. I watched, fascinated by this display, until its hand reached the outer limit of the octogram.

I expected a hum, or sparks, or some kind of glowing aura to manifest.

Instead, the nephilla took another step, the boards of the floor smoking beneath its fiery tread where within the confines of the summoning zone they had not.

I realised then my oversight, and panic gripped me.

The words spilled from my lips for I had practised them much and, though I had kept the paper handy for reading, knew them by rote.

'Too late,' the creature said with a voice like the crackle of a pyre. '*You cannot contain that which is already free. You might as well chain moonlight, foolish mortal.*'

I admit that I started to spout nonsense, condemning the nephilla back to the dark glade, calling upon such spirits of Caliban that I could remember to protect me. All of it was to no effect as the apparition walked calmly across the chamber to stand before me.

It bowed.

I stared in disbelief, agog at this expression of subordination.

'*You have called and answer has been given,*' the creature said to me, dripping fire to the boards like sparks from a collapsing log in the grate. In the moment my mind went to a ludicrous place and I found myself thinking that it had been wise to remove the rug, or we would have both been engulfed in the inferno.

The words of the nephilla finally sunk in and I recalled the conversation three decades earlier.

'Know thee of Erebus?' I said, amazed that the words of the summoned thing were so alike to those of the Word Bearer.

'*Slow you have been in coming to us,*' it replied. I thought then that it had not answered the question but I was so astounded, and more than a little pleased at what I had accomplished, that the ramifications of what it said did not occur to me.

'I wish to know of what passes beyond this world,' I said, thinking of the nephillic plane and the spirits within. The creature took me literally though, as it would often do if given the chance by imprecise questioning.

'*The galaxy burns,*' it told me, grinning, a tongue of fire licking across needle teeth of blue steel. *'The time of the Emperor draws to a close. The time of the Great Powers returns. All will be consumed and reborn in the fires of destiny.'*

It withdrew, walking back into the circle to stand at the centre like a dutiful destrier on a show ground. I had a thousand questions both practical and philosophical, but before I could utter the first syllable of interrogation the apparition guttered and disappeared, becoming a cloud of ash motes that fell to a grey layer within the octogram.

I laughed. I laughed hard, from relief and joy. I had done it. I had harnessed a power equal to the Lion and the Emperor. Greater, if the claims of the nephilla were to be true.

My thoughts passed back to the Knights of Lupus and how they had tried to release the same potential but had lacked the wisdom to do so. They had shackled the Great Beasts to their will and allowed the spirits of Caliban to sketch their realm in their dreams, but they had never succeeded in crossing the veil. Had they done so, they would have been paramount on Caliban and not the Order.

My gaze settled on the book that Erebus had given me, and I considered the words of the apparition. It seemed as though both Word Bearer and nephilla had been awaiting my ritual, like an elder loitering close to the door when a favoured grandchild is due to visit, eager to welcome them inside.

It did not occur to me that the power had not been mine. I had opened a door that was held ajar from within. I thought myself grand for succeeding at my first attempt, when the reality was that I had achieved nothing except self-delusion.

So it is with nephilla and their masters, especially the Architect of Fate. The balance of power is never certain and lies are so easily cloaked in the lightest truth. From that first encounter to the last on the eve of Caliban's death, I thought I was in control and forged a path for Caliban and the Order. In truth,

I was waylaid long ago by a false map and led like a fool into the most treacherous depths, from which I never freed myself.

It is always the way when dealing with the powers of the warp. Your first steps always seem to be in the right direction, but you will never know at what point you started following *their* road, because after a time you forget there was a destination at all, and all that remains is the journey.

Zapherael looked unconvinced and Luther sighed.

'The powers that seek to corral and corrupt us ask a simple question – what do you want?' said the former Grand Master. 'It may be complicated or simple, but we each have a desire within us that can be exploited. All of us. Even you.'

'You are the arch-corrupter!' Zapherael became very animated, flexing his fingers, spittle flying from his lips. 'You would spin this web of deception to misdirect us. You try to tell me the wrong thing, but couched in your lies is the truth. I know you placed your deceit in the thoughts of Morderan, lies he was forced to extinguish before they consumed him. The powers we face are long in their plots, seeding disaster generations before their wicked fruits ripen. Even as they tore the traitors from us they left you to sow discord on their behalf.'

'No!' Luther shook his head and fought the urge to advance, not wishing to come within striking distance of the angered Space Marine. 'The lure always changes, but the trap does not. The hardest road, the long road, is the only way to avoid their grip. Perhaps you have already travelled too far along the short path. Damnation or death, you must choose one or the other.'

'It is you that damned us to this perdition. Only our purity in exorcising the taint within our souls can deliver us from that act. Only the repentance of those that soiled the legacy of the Lion can expunge the curse.' A crazed gleam entered the eye of Zapherael, causing Luther to flinch. 'Do you repent,

Luther the Deceiver? Do you abandon your dark works and break from the corrupt masters you serve?'

Luther looked at the Space Marine and saw the derangement within him. It was the nature of their inculcation that they followed the Dark Angels creed above and beyond all other concerns. He had seen his interviewers hardening, becoming something different to what he had known to be a legionary. Inflexible.

That which could not bend would eventually break.

'Repent to me and I will release you,' Zapherael promised in a fierce whisper. 'Cleanse your soul and I shall return it to the void as a thing of purity.'

'Not to you,' Luther growled back, disgusted by the Dark Angel. He stopped short of voicing further argument, fearing it would become insult that would lead to physical retribution. This warrior was not a son of the Lion; his gain-brother would be appalled by such a display of ignorance and religiosity. 'There is only one that can hear my confession. The only one that I have betrayed. You call my followers the Fallen but you are the ones that have besmirched the legacy of Caliban and the Lion!'

'Traitor!' rasped Zapherael as he left, the curses of Luther following swiftly until stasis and the mind-journey returned.

TALE OF THE JAWS

Zapherael returned many times to lambast Luther and demand he seek forgiveness for his crimes against the Dark Angels. With each visit, Luther's resolve hardened, even as he started to lose himself amid the temporal stream again. His visions filled with images of the Lion – rather a giant warrior with a mane of blond hair and gleaming blade that he took to be the Lion – which convinced Luther that the primarch was still alive. He told Zapherael this fact, but rather than treat the news as the wondrous revelation it was, the Supreme Grand Master became even more angered.

'Do not think to excuse your treachery with these lies!' screamed the Space Marine when Luther once more refused to acknowledge Zapherael's authority to hear his confession. 'You slew the Lion and destroyed Caliban in revenge for the defeat of your master, Horus.'

No amount of argument would move Zapherael from this position, and he arrived the next time with several blades and hooks designed for the excruciation of flesh.

'You think you can bleed the truth from me?' Luther sneered.

'I will bleed the impurity from you and only the truth will remain. Our Interrogator-Chaplains have learned much with your followers as specimens. They were Space Marines, you are not. When your flesh is aflame with the agony of your sins, you will see the truth and admit to me that you are thrice-cursed. You turned on the Lion, you turned your back on the Emperor, and you treated with the Dark Gods.'

He ignored Luther's pleas for a more rational intercourse and instead bound him with chains; against his superhuman strength his prisoner's much-diminished physique gave him no opposition. With his implements of torture, he began to cut and tear, but Luther fled the pain into his dreams, his mind separating from his body to drift the rivers of time.

Only occasionally did he return to consciousness, to find his wounds tended or fresh injuries inflicted, and always faced the demand to repent of what he had done. Zapherael's delusion was contagious, passed on to the next to bear his title, and the next.

Sometimes bloodied, increasingly scarred, Luther's mind moved back and forth without control between the spiritual agony of his dreamworld and the physical pain of reality. Whatever injuries were inflicted on his body played out as terrifying nightmares of destruction and death in his visions. They became more hallucinatory, merging specific memories with great vistas of suns drowning in blood and worlds afire with war. He heard the tolling of bells in worship and then alarm, and saw million-strong columns of rag-clad humans baying and wailing, slashing themselves with small knives and flogging their own backs as they screeched their confessions to uncaring priests.

Their pain became his pain, and his pain became the Imperium's wails of agony as the wounds of Luther's flesh seemed visited upon the expanse of humankind. Pyres burned around effigies of the Emperor, consuming the impure. Luther watched immense buildings raised up with crenellated spires and soaring buttresses. From their great halls rang the voices of tens of thousands in war-prayer. Starships rained down death from orbit, scouring cities so that vertiginous temples could be built out of their ruins.

Over and over, screaming faces demanded that he repent, but their shouts were lost amid the death cries of billions. A fever gripped the galaxy and the Dark Angels were caught up with the insanity.

Until there came a cessation of pain. The absence of sensation was more confusing than the turmoil of his broken dreams, until Luther awoke, in a foetal crouch at the corner of the cell. A sharp stinging drew his attention to salves on the cuts across his chest and arms, fresh stitches in the wounds upon his face and back.

The chains were gone but a shackle about his ankle kept him linked to a ring in the wall.

He stared at the ruddied flagstones, dyed with his spilt blood. Lifting numb hands he saw he had no fingernails. His tongue probed at cracked teeth.

'Your will is more solid than the foundations of the Rock,' said a voice, making him flinch.

A Space Marine stood at the doorway, armoured in bone white, a black robe over the powered suit. He was bald, the nose thin and long, the lips fuller than Luther was used to seeing in his captors. He wondered if it had been his mania that had made the others look more akin to the Lion. Had he imposed his gain-brother's features onto his tormentors, or had the gene-seed that had run in the veins of the Dark Angels finally withered?

The Space Marine held a large cup in his hands and approached, putting it on the floor in front of Luther. The contents were clear.

'Water,' the Space Marine said.

'Rock? What rock?' Luther whispered.

'Hmm?' The Space Marine was taken aback by the question. With a broad wave of his arm he indicated everything around them. 'This place. This fortress-monastery. We call it the Rock.'

'It is a piece of Aldurukh, the only remnant of Caliban, I was told.'

'The only piece large enough to be worth keeping,' the man said. He nodded towards the cup. 'Drink.'

'The Imperium will burn,' Luther said, picking up the water. 'A madness will break it.'

'It has already begun,' the Space Marine said sadly. 'The great Church of the Emperor seeks dominion over all, yet worship is fractured and factions vie among themselves. A demagogue rules Terra in the Emperor's name, gathering ever greater power to himself. It has shone an unpleasant light on our own actions these last centuries. Even now, there are many among the Chapter that think we should pick one denomination or other to support.'

'The Church of the Emperor? You made Him a god?'

'*We* did nothing,' he said harshly. 'The rise of the Adeptus Ministorum has been millennia in the making. It is not for the Space Marines to dictate to the High Lords how they organise the Imperium, but when the Ecclesiarch is also the Lord of the Administratum that is too much power in the hands of one individual.'

'You do not believe the Emperor is a god? Perhaps you should.'

'We are relearning our faith, to put it into a different perspective. Our bonds to the Emperor are stronger than idolatry and a few sermons.'

Luther drank the water, smarting at its coldness in his ravaged mouth.

'Thank you,' he said, placing the cup exactly where it had been put before him. 'What is your name?'

'Tatraziel.'

'Why do you treat me differently? Do you not think I will repent?'

'I think the Supreme Grand Masters have spent too much time and effort on a broken, insane old man,' Tatraziel replied with a sorrowful shake of the head. 'Your confession is meaningless to me. It will not save one Dark Angel, nor bring one Fallen back from damnation.'

'Not even my damnation?'

'You are living your damnation, are you not?'

Luther bowed his head and said nothing, feeling the weight of the pronouncement heavy on his tortured frame.

'If you wish the Lion's forgiveness, you must earn it.'

Luther looked up, startled. He jumped to his feet, wincing as the stitches in his flesh pulled tight.

'The Lion lives? I told you! I told them all! Where is he?'

'I do not know if the Lion lives or has been dead these last five thousand years. He is gone, and has not returned. Too long we have wondered too much on the future and what might be, letting the present go astray. We overreached, as a Chapter and with you.'

'What did you mean when you said I have to earn the forgiveness of the Lion?' Luther's stomach cramped painfully, almost buckling him at the knees. He straightened, face twisted with discomfort. 'The water sits poorly in an empty stomach.'

'You have been too long starved, even for your altered physiology. I will bring a little food when we are done.'

'Why do you speak of the Lion's forgiveness?'

'Has it not occurred to you that perhaps you need to prove to the Lion that you repent of your deeds? Offer up those that strayed with you into the darkness and you will bring them and yourself back into the light.'

'Dark and light? Is your outlook so binary, Tatraziel of the Dark Angels?'

'Oh, I know the world of grey very well. People like you have dragged me into that realm between the moral and immoral. Now I find I must be a pragmatist, to be the bastion of reason when superstition and the madness of blind faith consumes others. You will help me or you will rot here. The Watchers will keep the stasis lifted and you will slowly die. Only when you are on the verge of expiring will they stop the flow of time again. So, I ask you, do you want to live out your damnation as you are now, or as a frail near-corpse?'

'You are just as vile as the others. Viler, for your civility and subtlety.'

'There is a renegade priest, Bucharis, who has taken rule of many, many worlds for himself, a rival to the Ecclesiarch of Terra. His sermons drag billions into false worship, fleets and armies serve his wishes above those of the High Lords. Our Librarians have discovered that one of his advisors is a follower of yours, named Machius.'

'Machius? That does not sound like a Calibanite name to me. I do not think he was of the Order.'

'He is listed in the manifests as a warrior of Caliban at the time of the Lion's return.'

'Many thousands were, but I cannot name them all.' Luther touched his nail-less fingers with the tips of his thumbs, feeling the rough skin, the scabbed blood. 'You can kill as many messengers as you like, it does not stop the message.'

'What does that mean? Is that a threat?' Tatraziel loomed closer. Luther shook his head.

'We had no gods or priests on Caliban. We took moral guidance from the old tales and our lords, and recreated the deeds of the best with our own lives.'

The greatest test of a knight was the quest. We were a martial people and for all that we treasured knowledge and lauded wisdom, a man or woman who took up arms was judged on that merit. If one wanted to be a carpenter or wainwright or incendriast, one would be apprenticed and submit a work for consideration to the master. So too the knightly route, save we called the youth a squire and the master *sar*, or mistress *sarl*. The masterpiece that would be judged was the slaying of a beast. Not any creature of the forests but a quest beast. A Great Beast.

Not all Great Beasts were the size of buildings and needed a squadron of knights to kill. Most were not, though they were no less a threat because of their smaller size. Nobody travelled alone. Caravans between settlements would transport goods and people, traversing the forests under the protection of a lord's knights or a troop of Wandered hired for the purpose. Livestock were raised in high-walled pastures, and messages sent by trained bird rather than herald.

It is better to think of the forests of Caliban as a treacherous sea, and the castles and forts of the people as islands among the green tides. Each stood alone, aware of its neighbours, communicating from afar but rarely interacting. Disputes over boundaries came about often simply because the shifting forest made measuring any meaningful territory almost impossible, so that bands of rivals would usually encounter each other only by mistake. Such skirmishes were brief and often resolved by contest of arms rather than actual battle to the death – knights were bound to one another even across settlements and to shed blood other than in the direct protection of one's liege or their servants was frowned upon. Of course, there were some bloodthirsty warriors and rulers, but they were the exception.

There were also a few lords that laid claim to larger areas, with subservient settlements about their townships, but for the most part the effort of policing and protecting these extended kingdoms was greater than the benefit. Nearly all such conquerors were vain men and women, beguiled by the tales of the dead kings from Old Night, who thought to unite several knightly realms beneath their banner. Such would-be monarchs were generally held in suspicion and almost always came to a bad end, whether by overstepping their authority and igniting revolution or by stoking the ambitions of more capable rivals.

Yet even a lord of such standing, whose realm stretched from dusk to dawn, could not credibly lay claim to reign over anything more than a kilometre and a half from any wall upon which they might stand. The forest ruled itself, and if it was a lord, the Great Beasts were its knights – hunters and protectors that would strike down those that crossed into their kingdom.

If there was one common factor across every settlement on Caliban, from the smallest hamlet to mighty Aldurukh, it was the ingrained respect and fear of the forest. From their earliest years, every Calibanite learned that the woods were death. Childhood tales abounded of those young rogues that wandered from the protection of their homes and met all manner of grisly ends. On Caliban there were no wandering foresters or hunters that would pluck the wayward child to safety at the last instant.

Which is to say that a quest was a remarkable thing. A knight would willingly ride into the forests to seek a quest beast. Sometimes they would find a trail to follow; more often they would travel from settlement to settlement, seeking news of a suitable quarry. Some quests took weeks, many lasted for a season and more. The most legendary quests lasted years, the knights that completed them returning as if from beyond the veil of death.

For there was another kind of tale we listened to as children, and like many others I am sure I paid more heed to these. They were the stories of the bravest knights of history, and the strange arboromancers, chanters, wood dragons and forest spirits they encountered. From within the high walls of Aldurukh, it was easy to dismiss the stories of boys and girls lost on trails to nowhere and remember instead Sar Candred who slew a dozen-headed snake, or the trials of Alistar of Nubrook and his encounter with the Sorcerarch of the Meadows. This was before I was sent to Storrock and witnessed the Horn of Ruin and other horrors. Between them these tales painted a picture of a realm replete with dangerous magic and fabulous glory – for it was always renown the hero gained, far more desirable than any coin or gems.

I was fourteen when I announced I would ride my quest. It was a precociously young age to do so, though my mother and father supported me without criticism. When I later became Grand Master and the Lion fought at my side, we changed recruitment to the Order to cope with the demands of those youngsters that wished to join us, but back then the only children raised within Aldurukh were born to parents that lived there, like I was.

We found it was more efficient to train adolescents as I had been trained, rather than rely on the vagaries of application from across Caliban, but I wonder if in trying to recreate my own remarkable rise we lost authenticity somewhere along the way. And even as I think of it, it seems to me that perhaps the Lion ordered things in a way that made it easier for us to be subsumed into the Legion when it arrived. Not consciously, but perhaps something of the creation of a legionary was imprinted in the primarch that pushed him to recommend our new recruitment practice.

But that was later. My master, Sar Elegor, thought me skilled enough, though raised question of my temperament. He spoke to me as we readied our destriers in the outer stable block. The spring tourney was due to start within the month and Sar Elegor had been drilling me and Accadis on the training fields.

'Tis no jaunt you are taking. You will leave Aldurukh and renounce everything that you have. All claims to title, rank and family are left at the gates. You can only return two ways. With the head of a quest beast...'

'Or as bones found in the wilds,' I finished with a laugh. 'I know well the tradition, Sar Elegor. I am ready, I swear it.'

'Perhaps you are, but there is no rush,' said Elegor.

'Winter has faded, summer will come swiftly,' I replied, cinching the broad belt about Accadis' girth. She turned her head to look at me, encouraging me to pull it tighter still. I did so. 'If I do not set out this year, I have only two seasons left before I depart to my gain-family.'

'So? They will be just as proud of you undertaking a quest as your birth parents.'

'But I want to quest as a squire of the Order,' I told him. I had not confided this before and he raised his eyebrows in doubt, so I explained. 'I know that none are born to the Order, but it would feel different if I were to bring back my quest prize to a place that was not Aldurukh.'

I could tell by his askance gaze that he thought this a vanity, so I continued.

'Not for *my* glory, but for the glory of the Order. I would set the head of the beast on the steps of the Angelicasta and make my oaths of knighthood to the Grand Master. Then, should I not prove worthy enough to return when I am an adult, at least my debt for raising me would have been paid.'

Elegor laughed, deeply and long, and slapped me on the shoulder so hard that he would have knocked me sprawling had I not been wearing my powered battle harness.

'I swear by the old glades that you are a dream, Luther,' he exclaimed. 'A more attentive student at arms I could not ask for. There is no manual of bladework, gunnery or tactics that you have not scrutinised to the smallest degree. In battlecraft, riding and hunting you are one of the finest squires to have graced the yards of Aldurukh.'

'So why do you laugh at me?' I asked.

'Any other boy or girl with your gifts might be accused of arrogance, in presuming that you can quest when so young. But you? You do it because you think you might not be worthy of coming back to the Order! You want to set out into the woods as a mere strip of a knight so that you can show your gratitude to the lord of Aldurukh!'

I saw then why he was amazed. I had thought nothing of my motives before, knowing only a restlessness that drove me to strive for each new achievement. I had seen the manner of warriors that had entreated the lord to be recruited to the Order and not found favour, and not one of them had been a coward or slouch. I said as much to my master.

'Nothing is certain, Luther, that is true,' he said, now laying a far gentler hand upon my shoulder as he spoke. 'The Grand Master does not permit gambling, but if I was of a mind to make wager, I would bet my armour, my steed, my quarters and my sword arm that you will come back to us as one of the most accomplished knights ever. Not because you deserve it, or some nonsense about destiny that I hear the others mutter, but because there is not another soul I know who would do more to *earn* that right.'

I was humbled by his words, and grateful, and nodded to show that I understood.

'Thank you,' I told him. 'But you know that I still mean to set off on my quest the day after the tourney is finished?'

'Of course you do,' Sar Elegor replied.

Which is what I did, having won laurels in four of the five events of the tourney, including Lord's Champion at the bolt gallery.

It is hard to describe the atmosphere that surrounds a young knight leaving to quest and it was not as I expected, though I had witnessed dozens during my childhood. It was different to be sat upon the mount rather than watching. As Elegor had pointed out, a knight on a quest no longer exists legally, having given up all rights and inheritances. If it sounds romantic, or morbid if you are of a pessimistic outlook, I can only say that it is practical. At least half of the knights that set out to slay a quest beast do not return, either through their untimely end or because they fail and give up. To wait months or years to learn of the fate of a departed questor, perhaps never to know it at all, would hugely complicate matters of succession, money and residence. Although such things were of small consideration within the Order, in the wider world the rule of law and the reign of lords depended upon such arrangements. And while Calibanites are not overly sentimental about family matters, we are not heartless and it is better to say one's farewells to a living relative and expect them not to return, than to see them off with a hope that may never be fulfilled.

Not all quests begin the same, and not all households treat them equally. Aldurukh even had fashions and expectations that changed over generations and depended as much upon the predilections of the current Grand Master as the noble traditions kept alive by the Lord Cypher.

As a squire I warranted little ceremony, and though many in Aldurukh thought highly of me and my chances of returning in glory, it would have been untoward for the Grand Master or any high dignitary to witness my passing. Instead my parents, Sar Elegor and a handful of companion squires assembled to see me through the gate.

Accadis sensed something of the occasion and was full of energy, eager to be leaving. I had painted over the device of Sar Elegor on her armoured flanks and the pauldrons of my wargear, breaking the master and squire bond that had existed between us. He gave me one of his bolt pistol magazines as a sign of his blessing, while the squires presented me with a garland of bright red flowers that they hung about my neck as though it were a medallion of the tourney.

'Bloodpetal,' Fyona told me in a whisper as she gave me a swift kiss on the cheek. 'To ward away blades.'

At a signal from Sar Elegor, the door within the great gate opened and I rode out onto Iorica's Causeway, the vastness of the forest spread around me as the road angled back and forth down the mountainside.

I told myself not to look back, but when I reached the first sharp bend in the causeway the toll of a bell rang down from the citadel. I recognised the note immediately, for it came from the Grand Voice, the bell whose knell rang out along the valley four times a day and could guide lost travellers to Aldurukh from kilometres away. It was not on the quarter-day so in my surprise I turned in the saddle.

It was then that a knot tightened about my heart, for on the tower of the causeway gate was a small group of knights. It was too far to see each of them, but above flew the long pennant of the Grand Master.

My nerve almost broke then, to think that the lord of Aldurukh had deigned to come to the wall and sound the Grand Voice for the passing of a squire. Accadis felt my reluctance and acted for me, rearing high with a loud snort before breaking into a canter that quickly took me around the switchback and out of sight of the wall.

My father had given me a silken cloth marked with the main landmarks west of Aldurukh, made during the most recent forays of the patrols in that direction. The westlands were more populous than other neighbouring realms, for the Sea of Alakon was only a few days' travel away and its waters were bountiful with fish. Some of the most famous knights had quested along those verdant shores and I hoped to emulate them in success.

Consulting this map, I left the causeway and passed under the canopy of the trees, the first time I had entered the forests alone.

My first destination was Ringate, an outer tower of the Order about sixteen kilometres from the causeway. I had spied the crag on which it sat as I descended, a grey finger amid the green, but once beneath the leaves I trusted more to Accadis' sense of direction than mine. I had a compass, of course, but the forests were littered with meteoric craters from the Starfire, when the planet had been bombarded with stellar debris for decades during Old Night. The needle was as likely to point towards some forest-swallowed deposit as it was north, and was of use only when utterly devoid of sight of sun or stars.

I was light of heart at first, as only a youth can be, and sang chansons to Accadis as she picked her way across the forest floor. Hearing my own voice, recounting the brave deeds of knights past, helped to steady my resolve. I thought of those brave warriors that had ridden out from Aldurukh and a thousand other fortresses across Caliban, and it gladdened me to count myself now among their number.

It was yet mid-spring and I had left not long after daybreak, so we had hours of good riding ahead. My pack and canteen were full, and though there was no road as such, I followed a trail used frequently by the patrols. If anywhere in the forests was safe, this was it, but as I sang, my eyes scoured the forest and my hand stayed near the pistol holstered at my saddle bow.

The sun was not yet at its zenith when I came upon a cleared path and saw the peak of Ringate above the trees ahead. A single rider awaited me at the gate and introduced herself as Galass, a squire from further south who had also recently begun her quest. The warden of Ringate, having been already notified of my similar intent, had bid Galass to remain a few days until my arrival, that we might be companions for a time.

I was reluctant, I must admit. I could relate half a dozen

tales of pairs and bands of knights questing together, for there was nothing in law or lore to forbid it as long as the prize was suitably impressive or each knight brought home a head. But the tales that had enamoured me most as a child had been of the singular questor and their individual travails against world and beast.

I could not admit as such before Galass, so we agreed to ride together as far as Alakside, the largest town on the eastern shore of the inland sea. It was four days' travel and I thought that once there she would depart my side and I could continue alone in the finest tradition.

As it transpired, Galass was admirable company. Hailing from a smaller fortress than I, she was full of questions about life around the Angelicasta and the Order. In return, she was a font of strange tales from the forest, some so outlandish I wondered if any of her stories were true. She laughed quickly and often, almost childish sometimes in her delight at small things, though as the Terrans would reckon it she was three years my senior.

Galass was also no amateur with a blade. I had thought my training by the knights of the Order unmatched, but her bladecraft showed her to be my equal, though I was the more accurate with bolt pistol. Her experience of the woods showed often, more than three years' difference would account. She had a sense for its moods, even though we were far from the lands where she had learned to ride and hunt.

Spring was a time of divide. Prey was plentiful for hunter and beast alike, and so one could travel without too much fear of malice from the indigenous predators, unless one happened upon a Great Beast. In their stead, the forest itself was peril enough, for in the rising of the sap and the budding of seedlings the plants were swiftly waking from their dormancy and alert to intruders. West of Ringate the trees were young and feisty, so that one might swear they lifted root or lowered branch to waylay us. Fanciful, yes, but there was always a presence in the forests, a sense of constant watchfulness that was not attributed to a single bird or beast, but the whole arboreal entity.

We taught each other songs as we rode, so that Galass learned the chansons of the Order's past Grand Masters and from her I recited songs that she claimed would placate the spirits of the forests: verses of leaf and bough, grass and sun and the animus that lived within them.

We reached Alakside without incident and I had changed my mind on the wisdom of parting. Within Aldurukh one is never more than a bow shot from another person, even in the dungeons or towers of the Angelicasta. The thought that I might have spent the last few days alone chilled me, so I asked Galass if she was willing to travel further with me. She said she would answer the next day, which surprised me as I had just assumed she would want to continue at my side – though she kept her smile, she reminded me that I was part of her quest as much as she was part of mine. For a somewhat self-centred teenager, that was an important lesson and one which I have tried to keep in my heart ever since. We each are only guests in the lives of others.

In the morning she arrived with Kirl, a local guide and tracker. Of middle age, Kirl claimed to have accompanied half a dozen knights on their quests over the years. Galass told me that before leaving Ringate, she had been advised to enquire for a scout at the House of Garell, and it was they that had recommended Kirl.

The three of us took a ferry across the river mouth where Alakside sprawled along the shore, and after Kirl conversed with several fisherfolk and other locals she announced that we should continue northwards following the coast.

'The coast?' Galass asked as we rode out of the north gate of the town, the shadows of noon short on the ground, the sun hot for the season. 'Are we to crawl from fisher hut to fisher hut inspecting crab pots for our quarry?'

Her tone was light but I could see that her words rankled with Kirl.

'You can head straight into the elderwood if you like, child,' the guide replied sharply, pointing east from the small stretch of road that led from the gate. 'Fen and beasts in equal measure for those that are stupid enough.'

'Stupid?' Galass scowled at Kirl, the first time I had seen anything like anger in her features. 'At least I am not cowardly, soiling myself at the thought of meeting a Great Beast. No quarry of worth comes this close to the shore, unless you count those in the waters, but I would not switch my mount for some swaying skiff to hunt one.'

'Let us cool our tempers,' I suggested. 'We are freshly met and still strangers. We should decide nothing in anger or haste.'

'At least one of you has a brain between their ears,' said Kirl, hearing me but not heeding my words.

'Who are you to speak to me like that?' cried Galass, and for a heartbeat I thought she would strike our new companion.

'Who are you that I shouldn't?' Kirl replied archly. 'A squire? A lord's daughter, maybe?'

'We are nothing,' I said quickly. 'We are on the quest. No titles, no ranks, no homes.'

My interruption silenced Galass, and she glowered at me for several seconds.

'By the heartfire, you really are annoyingly humble, Luther,' she said eventually, shaking her head. She turned her attention back to our guide. 'My apologies, Kirl. Is there some middle ground between us? Somewhere close to the elderwood we can venture?'

'If you wish me to guide you, we head north,' said Kirl. 'Those are the lands I know. Plenty enough danger for you.'

'See?' Galass turned her dark eyes back to me, lip curled. She said nothing but kicked her heels to the flanks of her destrier and rode ahead, cutting eastwards off the road.

'You brought Kirl to me!' I shouted after her, but she disappeared into the trees without a backward glance. I looked at Kirl with a shrug. 'It seems your service was short-lived, I hope you have had coin enough to cover your time.'

'You're going after her?' said the guide. She sighed and pulled her smaller steed closer. 'The going should be fine for three days east, but then you will strike the edges of the Shadow-mire. You'll know it because the name is well earned. Go south there, back towards the mountains. You'll find firmer ground, and if you carry on you'll come to Lords Fayre after another day. Find another guide there, please. Do not go into the marsh-lands, whatever tempts you onward. It is a queer place, thick with the spirit of the woods. Take care, Luther. That one, she is more dangerous than any beast you will find.'

I thanked her for her advice and urged Accadis after Galass, plunging into the greenery in her wake.

The land about was certainly stranger than either of us had known, though we were still within sight of the great peak where Aldurukh nestled when we came upon a break in the trees. The ground was soft beneath the tread of our destriers, the trees spread out with large patches of trailing bushes and ferns between. The sun broke regularly through the canopy and the ride was pleasant, though we remained alert.

My conversations with Galass took a different turn, and she spoke more of her family – her ancestors specifically. As Kirl had alluded, Galass was a child of higher nobility, and being devoid of siblings there was much pressure on her to complete her quest and be ready to take up her role as heir to the lordship. For her part, she was set on becoming a knight of the Order, much to the dismay of her mother and father.

As she spoke, it became clearer to me that she did not see her knighthood as a duty so much as a right. A birthright, in fact, owed to her for claiming noble lineage for a dozen generations. Yet in her recounting of her family past there seemed something amiss, for she spoke much of their quests and victories, but very little about where they ruled or the people they commanded.

We camped as soon as the sky started to darken, splitting the overnight watch between us. The forest was alive with movement and calls through the night, and for the next two as we continued towards the ill-regarded Shadowmire. The further we rode, the more we had the sense that we were heading downhill, as though the whole forest was descending into some broad valley. The skies greyed overhead and the ground became spongy, the trees thinning with each passing kilometre.

Here and there we came upon fragments of masonry, most almost lost amid the moss and leaves, some of them large stones easily the size of a cart, swallowed by centuries of growth. Galass fell silent and her expression was grave. It seemed to me that she knew something of what had been here; a sadness passed over her face when we came upon what was clearly a toppled column or creeper-wreathed gateway.

'There was a settlement here, a large one,' I said to her, reining Accadis to a stop next to a half-buried slab. The stone looked odd, too uniform in its texture, free of vein or grain. I look back with the knowledge of ferrocrete and know that it was something similar, but at the time I just thought it unnatural.

'A city,' she said quietly, continuing on.

I rode after her, the trailing weeds plucking at the ankles of our steeds as they forged through the greenery. The clouds had thickened more, threatening rain, but there was barely a breath of wind to stir the stillness and it was clammy rather than cool.

'Is this where your forefolk came from?' I asked. 'Did they live here? Is that why you were so insistent on coming?'

'Yes, these were the lands of my ancestors,' she told me. 'It was called Greyhome, older even than Aldurukh. This is probably one of the border keeps. There used to be roads as well, but the marsh has long swallowed them too.'

'I do not think there will be much to see. Further in, I mean,' I said to her, pointing to the part-swallowed ruins. 'But we can look anyway.'

'Venture into the Shadowmire?' She looked at me as though I had declared we ride across the Sea of Alakon.

'Was that not what you wanted?' I laughed. 'Your argument with Kirl?'

'I...' She seemed disturbed by the thought. 'I wanted to hunt a beast on our old lands, not lose myself in the haunted marshes. Greyhome was cursed, devoured by the forest, the people forced to flee.'

It sounded fanciful, like many of her tales.

'There are lost towns throughout the forests, that were abandoned to the encroachment of the trees,' I said. 'Sometimes the forest just gets too strong to hold back year after year.'

'This was not a slow decline, Luther,' Galass said, her eyes fixed on me with a fearful look. 'This was an attack, the ire of Caliban roused to overwhelm the city with an assault of beasts and plants. A sorcerer called Ezrekiel had demanded fealty of my forebears and they had him imprisoned. The next night, the walls were torn apart by the limbs of rampaging trees while nephilla and Great Beasts raced through the streets slaughtering all.'

I tried to take her story seriously, but she read the doubt in my eyes.

'The River Erewater broke its banks and flooded the ruins, and what had once been a great hill became a swamp,' she continued, angered by my scepticism. 'Even the skies are filled with permanent storm clouds as a reminder of Ezrekiel's wrath.'

I think back to the stories of my childhood and wonder why I found it hard to believe Galass' account even when I had been raised on tales of sorcery and valour. I suppose it was difficult to connect those legends with someone right in front of me. A defiant part of me wanted to show her there was nothing mystical about this place, it was just a result of Caliban's perpetually changing mood and landscape.

'If we are to create a worthy story, we might as well make it the grandest possible,' I said to her. 'Think of when future squires recount the tale of Luther and Galass, and how they dared the ghost-shrouded swamp to hunt the quest beast that had made its lair in her ancestral lands. You may not be able to reclaim Greyhome from the fens, but you can take back its glory.'

Did I mention I have a gift with words that can sway the hardest heart?

She thought about this and I could see fear become desire in her face. She reached out a gauntleted hand, fist clenched, and I banged mine atop it in knightly agreement.

'There is something not right though,' she said, her smile returning for the first time since we had parted company with Kirl. 'Surely the bards will sing of Galass and Luther, not the other way around!'

We rode onwards.

I had thought Kirl's warning about the boundary of the Shadowmire had meant the scattered ruins, but before midafternoon that day her meaning became much clearer. The forests had given way to fenland except for tree-clad hillocks breaking up through the mud every kilometre or so, their crowns topped with the nubs of ancient buildings.

The ground went from soft to wet over the course of a few kilometres, until our destriers were plucking their hooves from ankle-deep sludge, their breathing becoming laboured. As best we could, we rode from one mound to the next, taking a circuitous route at times to stay upon the driest land. To make matters worse, the immense bowl into which we descended was filled with tatters of fog, reducing our view to just a couple of hundred paces ahead, the hills by which we navigated rendered into sketches of distant shadow.

It was then that I had my first misgivings, but Galass now seemed intent on our new plan and I did not wish to appear frightened. It was still some time before dusk, but the cloud was thick and the sun weak, and we decided to make camp on a hilltop while we still had some light to see by. We found a hilltop that was relatively dry and broad, and having tethered our steeds to the twisted trees that populated its summit, set about building a fire and rough shelter.

A drizzle began to dampen our mood further, replacing the banks of fog with a steady haze of falling water. As best we could, we strung our oilskins between three trees and sheltered with our steeds, eating our supper cold. Is it not odd that the old tales never mentioned the discomfort of sleeping in sodden gear, nor the indignities of attending to one's bowel movements amid pouring rain? I was certainly starting to feel that perhaps my optimism and confidence had got the better of me.

It was Galass' turn at watch first but it took some time for me to sleep, water pattering on the roof of our bivouac, the trickle of freshly made rivulets running past. I eventually slept fitfully and was woken by a heavy snorting from the destriers at the same time as a hand touched my shoulder.

Opening my eyes I looked up into a clear, star-filled sky. It was beautiful. It was rare to see such a sight, for in Aldurukh the smog of fire and furnace and the light of the wall lamps made stargazing difficult, while the forest canopy obscured the view of the night for most of the land outside the mountains.

Galass' grip on my shoulder tightened, pushing the pauldron

into my flesh, while the grumbling of the steeds grew more insistent.

Sitting up, I saw that she was gazing down the hillside, as were the destriers. A fog had seeped up from the muddy waters, creating the impression that we sat on a mountaintop amid the clouds. There was another sort of beauty there, peaceful rather than grandiose, but I had no mind to appreciate it for I saw immediately what had disturbed my companions both human and equine.

Shadows moved through the mists.

Riders in single line, followed by others on foot. Silhouettes moving from west to north about half a boltfall from where we looked down. I could tell immediately that we had spied something ethereal for there was not the slightest noise. No tread of foot, splash of hoof or jingle of harness.

A cold breeze touched my cheek but did not stir the leaves on the stunted trees, nor tousle the manes of our steeds.

'The dead of Greyhome,' whispered Galass, trembling beside me.

I was shaking too as I reached for the pistol in the pile of belongings I had used as a pillow. Slipping it from its holster, I stood up.

'You think you can shoot a wraith?' whispered Galass, grabbing my arm. 'These are not quest beasts!'

We watched the spectral warriors glide through the mists, heading deeper into the marshes. I could see nothing of them but vague outlines, like shadows cast upon the mist. As each passed I expected a head to turn towards us, to see us standing in dread at the hilltop, to issue some ghastly cry of alarm.

But we were not seen, and I thought perhaps the ghosts were not there at all. Or maybe just a memory, imprinted on the land about Greyhome, replaying when starlight and fog were in correct conjunction.

It must have been minutes but it felt like hours, until the last of the apparitions faded into the fog. We stayed still for longer, eyes trying to peel back the mist, imagining that the spectral column would return.

Neither of us slept again that night. Though at times my eyelids were as heavy as lead, the moment they fluttered closed I thought I felt the icy touch of some ghast on my skin and I would be wide awake again. Even so, when the first orange smudge of dawn started to gleam in the mists it felt like waking up from a dream, so unreal had been the encounter.

We readied ourselves and our steeds in silence, neither of us with a hunger for breakfast. The early morning sun dispelled much of the fog, revealing a high mound on the horizon to the north, topped with a scattering of trees and broken walls.

'That must be Greyhome,' I said, taking Accadis' reins to lead her down the hill. 'We could be there by noon.'

'Not I,' said Galass. Her eyes were bloodshot, her brown skin darker still around them, as though it had been many nights since she had slept. 'I have seen enough of Greyhome and my ancestors. The darkness dwells there now, even after many centuries. Let us return to the forests and hunt like knights.'

'What of the Tale of Galass and Luther? Are they to say that we dared the Shadowmire but were baulked? The ghosts have gone and if they were not some trick of tired imaginations then they intended us no harm. Come on, we shall be back to this camp before sundown, I promise.'

'You promise?' Her laugh was as cold as the ethereal touch in the night, and cut sharper than my chainsword. 'Kirl was right, I was wrong. This is no place for two squires. My ancestors barely escaped these fens, I will not give them a second chance to end my line. The spirit of Ezrekiel knows my blood – I can feel his presence in every root and ripple, seeking me, hungering for those that escaped his wrath.'

With that, she mounted her steed and started precipitously back down the mound, retracing our steps of the day before.

'South!' I shouted after her. 'Keep the rising sun on your left!'

I cannot say whether she did not hear me or ignored me, but she continued on to the west. I watched for a short while, highly tempted to follow. But my own words came back to admonish me. Would the bards sing of how the brave Sar Luther ran away from a half-dreamt ghost rather than daring the bones of the ancient city? I had vowed to return to Aldurukh to honour the Order, and I would do so with a tale that would be remembered for an age.

Such is the stupidity of youth.

At least Accadis seemed willing to stay with me, and I mounted when we reached the weed-choked waters. Northwards she plodded, slow and purposeful, making sure of her footing with each step. By mid-morning the clouds had gathered again. Little of the sunlight reached us through the haze, and I lost sight of the mound of Greyhome. Even so, we pressed on as straight as possible, my steed sometimes plunging belly-deep into the pools and pushing up the muddy banks with loud snorts. They might have been effort alone, but I started to imagine an air of complaint about her exhalations.

My earlier optimism faded as the morning passed, even as the light of the sun faded too. I judged it midday at least but there seemed no solidifying of the ground beneath Accadis' hooves and no sign of an upward slope that would mark our ascent to the old city. I started to sing, as I had done before, but now my voice seemed flat, dissipating into the nothingness to be received by unwelcome silence. Croaks and creaks of disturbing kind sounded to either side, and unseen things splashed into the waters.

I found myself turning in the saddle often, expecting to see something behind me. I hoped it would be Galass, having found her courage, but dreaded to see a more ethereal rider. Yet there was neither living nor dead, just the emptiness of the fog haze that swirled from the warming pools. I carried my pistol in my hand, reassured by its weight, as much as anything could bolster my weakening nerve.

It was then that I drew most heavily on the lessons of my mentors. 'Bravery,' I told myself and Accadis, 'is not the absence of fear but to overcome it.'

Had I been walking, I suspect I may have turned back, or veered aside, but Accadis trod purposefully onwards. I abandoned any notion that we would return to the bivouac we had made, even if I believed we could find it again. Instead I planned to make camp amid the ruins ahead, the moment we found firm land.

As seeming reward for my positivity the going became easier for Accadis, and in the gloom ahead I spied a larger darkness that was the slope of the great mound. The destrier sensed it too, straining to move on. I was not yet ready to give her free rein, for there was still ample treachery to be found in the muddy slope ahead.

'Patience,' I told her, leaning forward to holster my pistol and use my free hand to pat her neck.

The marsh to our left exploded, throwing mud and water over us. Accadis whinnied and bucked. The rein only in one hand, my weight ill-balanced, her sudden panic hurled me from the saddle. I swung from the rein and splashed down into the filth. I spluttered, the mud and weeds dragging at my attempts to pull myself free even as Accadis shrieked again, a most terrifying and unnatural noise.

Blinded by mud, I fumbled forward, trying to find saddle or stirrup. Something was thrashing through the water, which was about thigh-deep on me as I stood up. Accadis was beyond my reach, with my pistol on the saddle still, and my chainsword also.

My foot caught on what I took to be a weed or root and I fell forward, but it was not soft marsh bed that my hand struck but something harder yet yielding. A sudden pain flared through my leg and I flailed out of the silt, gasping down air and water in equal amount. Choking, I scraped the mud from my face and then bellowed as the pain in my ankle became an agony and I felt barbs burying deep to the bone.

I realised that it was no thorn-twist that had seized me, but some creature of the marsh. Red swirled amid the brown water and my assailant pulled again, trying to drag my leg from underneath me. My other foot slipped and I twisted as I fell, the water breaking my fall as I landed atop the creature.

I felt it release my leg, but my relief was short-lived. Half a dozen sharp teeth sank into the inside of my wrist, piercing flesh between the vambrace of my harness and the palm of my gauntlet. Some power smiled upon me at that moment, for had those fangs entered by a fraction more then surely an artery or tendon would have been severed. Either would have been death, through blood loss or being rendered defenceless.

I pounded at the dark shape with my other fist, driving the studded knuckle of my gauntlet repeatedly into whatever I could see, even as the beast pulled me down into the mire. The water splashed up into my open mouth as I shouted, choking me again, and as I retched, my attacker renewed its attempts to drown me, circling behind me with my arm in its jaws, turning me over so I was face down in the murk. Blinded and starved of air, fearing that to rip myself free of its grip might well tear away my hand, I sought some soft part to jab or squash with my free hand.

My panic grew as I felt the water deepening, the sanctuary of the shore seeming to slip away even though it was I that was moving, dragged back into the marsh. I tried to turn and kick but instead entangled myself with water plants.

This proved to be a boon, as the strength of the creature was tested against the roots of the binding weed, with my body as the link between them. Though I was but an adolescent, I had been trained daily since the days I first walked, and my body was lean and muscled, augmented by the rudimentary systems of my harness. As a squire I had not yet earned full powered armour, but my half-suit still contained systems to boost my strength.

Unfortunately, my lungs would give out before my muscles, unable as I was to draw breath or turn to my back.

A sudden renewed thrashing made me think a second attacker was incoming, and I feared death was but moments away. Something heavy parted the water nearby, the wave lifting me and my assailant together. As oxygen starvation made stars dance in my vision, I waited for the clamp of new jaws on leg or throat or midriff.

Instead there was another mighty splash and I felt my wrist let go. Flexing, I was able to break the surface, heaving down a long breath before crying out in pain.

I could barely see. I felt my cloak pulled, dragging me backwards. I thought it was my foe, but as I twisted to find some way to attack, I saw instead the welcome bulk of Accadis. With fabric between her teeth she pulled me towards the shore, which I saw now was still only a few metres away. In my dread I had thought myself hauled into the terrible depths of the marshland.

Snorting, my destrier made drier ground, pulling me for at least a hundred metres until we were well clear of the water. As I gasped and coughed on hands and knees she stood guard beside me, pacing back and forth as though a sentry patrolling a wall.

Eventually I fell to my back, chest heaving. I cried, weeping tears of terror and relief together. Accadis nuzzled me then for comfort, and her warm breath was as welcome as blanket or fire in a gale.

Though all was swathed in gloom from the clouds I could tell that night was coming swiftly. I was just about able to stand on my bad leg and could use my injured hand well enough, and awkwardly bound both with bandages from my packs. As with our last campsite, there seemed no piece of dry wood for a fire and I had not the strength even to bend a sapling to make a roof. Looking up the slope, I could see the broken remnants of Greyhome's walls and scattered masonry that must have been outworkings, but realised I no longer had any desire to venture into the ruins.

I found the toppled remains of a wall a few metres away, enough that in the lee of it there was dry ground, though still nothing that would take a flame. Accadis continued further along the slope, cropping at the sporadic patches of weeds and grass. My body felt flushed out in the aftermath of my dread, so that even the dull ache in my wrist and ankle was not enough to keep sleep from stealing over me as I sat feeling dejected and lost.

Movement in the bushes woke me.

It was by now pitch-black and I heard a snuffling noise accompanied by the rustle of leaves and scratch of displaced twigs. I thought it might be Accadis returning but heard no heavy footfall nor loud breath that I would have expected.

I slipped my hand to the pistol I had wisely taken from my saddle holster, but could see barely my hand in front of my face, never mind a target further away. With my back to the crumbling wall I slowly stood, still hearing the approaching disturbance, now no more than six or seven metres away but as invisible to me as the air itself.

The scuffling stopped and I heard a sharp inhalation a little to my right. I adjusted my aim to where I guessed the creature was but held my fear in check, forcing myself not to shoot until presented with a definite mark.

I got one a few seconds later when something erupted from the nearby scrub, just a shadow darker than the night.

In the flare of the bolt's firing I saw jaws wide, rows of finger-length teeth gleaming in the stark yellow light. Dark scales, black or green perhaps, still slick from the marsh waters. Eyes of black reflecting a pinprick of muzzle flash.

My bolt hit, somewhere along the beast's flank. I heard the thump of the second detonation and the thing shrieked and flinched. Even so, I had no time for a second shot: the creature was almost at my legs again.

I turned and ran, darting to my left as it flung itself over the last metres. My armour whined as it assisted my hurried steps, trying to replicate my panicked movements. In my haste I forgot my training, the slightly loping stride one must adopt so that the armour can work efficiently. Instead the servos stuttered and shook, almost staggering me.

My gasping breaths did not hide the crash of foliage around and behind me, and I thought that I had more than one pursuer. Knowing the beast was equally deadly in the water I instinctively angled up hill, running diagonally up the slope. Here my armour was of more use, boosting my slower strides so that I nigh leapt from fallen stone to fallen stone, and bounded over broken tree trunks and toppled logs.

I pulled out my knife as I ran, more to slash at any entangling limb of a trailing plant than as a weapon against my assailant. A few dozen strides further up the hill I stumbled, my knee smashing into something unseen in the darkness that sent me spinning sideways. I felt something hard beneath my hand and knee, though covered with moss and filth. Flagstones, I thought, or more of the strange featureless stone we had seen in the outskirts.

In desperation rather than bravery, I turned towards my attacker and lit the lamp of my suit. Pale light sprang out into the night, illuminating the slope and the twisted trees that littered it. The bushes about twenty metres away moved violently and I raised my pistol again, taking in a deep breath to calm myself.

The thing that burst from the broad leaves was the size of a dog, barely as big as a mastiff. Confused, thinking it a different creature, I did not open fire, wary of another beast perhaps circling around. Yet in the light of the lamp it was clear that this was my attacker. The jaw was long, filled with teeth disproportionately large to the rest of its body. I saw my blood flecked on the scales of its face.

I almost laughed as I opened fire, putting a bullet into its mouth as it opened its jaws to attack. The bolt entered its throat before detonating, almost ripping off the head. The creature skidded through the mulch a few metres away, back legs twitching for a few seconds longer until it fell still.

The silence that followed was excruciating, as I expected all manner of creatures to descend upon me, drawn by the noise and the light. I was still not wholly convinced that the thing dead before me was the same that had attacked me in the marsh, but I noted the tail was like the flukes of a whale and the feet were webbed, ideal for a watery hunter. Its speed over the ground had been impressive too.

A loud thudding announced the arrival of Accadis, who must have been some distance away to have arrived so late to the fight. She whinnied and shied away from the corpse, shaking her head. There was no doubt that the creature was touched by the spirit of Caliban, but I could not in any confidence call it a Great Beast.

I patted Accadis on the neck, comforting myself as much as her, and stroked her flank as I looked at the creature that had so terrorised me. I wondered whether if I had been with Galass it would have attacked at all. Certainly if I had first come upon it on the land and in the light, I would not have thought twice about the confrontation. My fear was greater than I had ever imagined, but I was too young to realise what that meant. I laughed at my foolishness rather than learned the lesson of my experiences confronting the weakness within my soul.

'Our quest is not over yet, my friend,' I told Accadis, turning away from the beast with the terrible jaws.

'It was several more months before I found a quest beast worthy of the title,' Luther concluded, his gaze distant as he remembered the encounter. With a blink, he focused on Tatraziel again. 'I returned to Aldurukh with my prize as I had promised, and was later made knight by the Grand Master on the morning of my coming of age, then departed to my gain-parents that noon. But it wasn't until much later, when I was reunited with Sar Elegor, that I realised the true purpose of the quest.'

'And you're going to enlighten me?' said Tatraziel. 'I assume there is some moral to this meandering tale. I ask about Machius and you spin a story about a beast in the marsh.'

'You never asked about Galass.'

'The other knight? What of her?'

'I do not know,' Luther said sadly. 'She never came to the Angelicasta. She may have died, or given up, or simply returned to her settlement to rule as her father intended. Seeing the ruins of Greyhome and the ghosts of her ancestors certainly scared her even more than the beast of the jaws scared me.'

'And that's the lesson?' Tatraziel looked disappointed. 'The real enemy is in our own minds? I have read many of your earlier words and I think you are nothing but a cheap storyteller. Not so much one of the lords or sorcerers from the tales of the Wandered, but one of the beggar-bards yourself.'

Luther laughed.

'I cannot argue otherwise, because plainly I have not made my point clear. You see, as a knight the test is not whether you can slay a dangerous beast. My lord knew my skill at arms before I set foot beyond the gate. It is not even whether one has courage, or stamina, or wisdom to persist in the quest. Some quests are a matter of days, little test at all.'

Tatraziel's expression changed from scepticism to suspicion, his eyes narrowing.

'The test is in leaving the castle,' said the Supreme Grand Master. 'To give up all that came before and begin again with nothing.'

Luther nodded and smiled.

'You are a better audience than most of your predecessors.'

Tatraziel said nothing for several minutes and Luther helped himself to more water from the jug the Space Marine had set down in the cell.

'Our bonds to our homes restrict us,' muttered Tatraziel. 'Our families are a distraction. If we are to focus solely on what must be done, we cannot carry the weight of what we were born with. To be a Dark Angel is the beginning and the end.'

Luther frowned as he listened, his misgivings growing as Tatraziel continued his whispering.

'You misunderstand,' said Luther. 'I mean that you must set behind all in your past. The Legion cannot become what it needs to become unless it starts anew.'

'Indeed!' said Tatraziel. 'When the last of the Fallen has repented we shall close that chapter of ancient history forever. And to do so, we must be dedicated to the hunt beyond all else. Our past lives, where we come from, mean nothing. Caliban is gone, there is no home but the Rock.'

Luther groaned and shook his head, but before he could protest, Tatraziel was heading for the door.

'No more stasis!' Luther begged, running after the Space Marine, but his pleas fell on ears deaf to them as the door swung shut.

TALE OF THE HUNT

Tatraziel did not come back, but a succession of others did. Amathiel, Duremis, Hazrael, Tyrhis, and then Anaziel. Luther concentrated as best he could on each, learning their mannerisms, dislikes and predilections. He tried to engage them more, to learn from them even as they learned from him. It was difficult, for even within stasis his mind continued to move, albeit with glacial slowness. The visions returned in sporadic fashion, but Luther was able to identify them as such and came to recognise the signs of their imminent arrival. Coming out of stasis often triggered a brief episode, so that despite his efforts to remain conscious and sane during his interrogations, more often than not he would experience several minutes of temporal disorientation first.

Always they wanted know about his followers, the ones they had called the Fallen. He tried to help as best he could, from what scattered intelligence he gained from his uncontrollable forays into the future. A few he knew by name from Caliban, but could advise little on their current plans or whereabouts.

Decade by decade, century by century, his life continued in brief episodes and he gleaned what he could from his interrogators about the galaxy beyond his prison. In time it all blurred into a single unending story of decline, brief resurgence, crisis and war. Luther wondered if it seemed this way because they came to him only when in need but eventually he was forced to concede that whatever the Emperor's plans had been for His Imperium, they most definitely had gone awry a long time ago.

The way the Space Marines talked about the Emperor was confused as well. They venerated Him, speaking His name as an all-powerful being, but also spoke of His sacrifice, as though He were dead. With each generation of Dark Angels it was clear that the grip of blind tradition grew, the reason and Enlightenment of the Imperial Truth no longer even a distant memory, their changing character revealed through Luther's stark bursts of acquaintance with their line of commanders.

Luther was sometimes able to warn them of coming tragedy, but it was hard to act upon passing glimpses of destruction, to locate the demagogue that stirred war or the alien fleet lurking in the shadow. Not once did they thank him, though he tried his utmost to oblige their questions as best he could. Their interrogations were always rooted in the false notion that the Fallen were still acting to some grand plan Luther had created in the last days of the Order. Whenever he tried to disabuse his captors of this notion, he was accused of further deceit.

The routine changed with Anaziel, or more specifically with Orias, for it was the first time any Dark Angel had come to him accompanied by one other than the Watchers in the Dark. So shocked was Luther that he thought he was caught between the present and some future sight, the one overlapping the other.

'Apologies, Master Anaziel, but I am at odds with myself today,' said Luther when the nausea of stasis-slip had faded. He rubbed his eyes and squinted at the apparition of the second Space Marine. 'I think I am temporally dislocated once more.'

'This is Grand Master Orias,' said Anaziel. 'My finest captain and soon to be Chapter Master.'

'I...' Luther was at a loss what to think. 'I have never been introduced to a successor before. As I recall, one does not simply stand down from the position of Supreme Grand Master. It is, if you'll excuse the expression, a position inherited post-mortem.'

'Not Supreme Grand Master,' said Orias, stepping closer. He looked older than Anaziel, a grey beard close-cropped to chin and cheeks, hair swept back by a band. 'Just Grand Master. I am to lead a new founding, the Disciples of Caliban. Anaziel thought my particular objective warranted learning of your existence, though I will be the first and last of my Chapter to know of it.'

'It sounds like I should be flattered,' laughed Luther. 'I did not realise I was so important.'

'You are our darkest secret, Luther,' Anaziel said heavily. 'Only by the journals of the Supreme Grand Masters and the guidance of the Watchers does anyone know of you. Only one has guarded that knowledge.'

'Until now?' said Luther. 'What has changed?'

'Nothing, and that is the problem,' said Anaziel. 'We chase the Fallen. We catch some, others elude us. Some repent, many do not. We break open their schemes and extract their secrets, and yet we are no closer to learning what they intend.'

'Seven thousand years since Caliban died,' said Orias. 'Yet there are more Fallen than ever.'

'The Order numbered more than thirty thousand on Caliban,' said Luther. 'And from what I have heard, they were scattered in time as well as space, much like my thoughts. The last of them may not come to light for another seven thousand years.'

'Which is why we need a more definitive strategy,' said Anaziel. 'We cannot just react, we must actively seek the enemy.'

'And that is your task?' Luther looked at Orias. 'The hounds of the hunt? You are going to round up the rest of the Order?'

'No, the Hunt for the Fallen remains the pursuit of all the Dark Angels and our successors,' said Anaziel. 'That is a task beyond a single Chapter. The Disciples of Caliban have a singular role in addition to their duties to the Imperium.'

'We're going to hunt down and capture Cypher,' declared Orias, with more confidence than Luther thought was warranted. 'Your protestations no longer fall on deaf ears, Luther. We do not think you are the architect of the Fallen's plans.'

'The Lord Cypher is?' Luther said.

'To some extent. As far as any is in command. Cypher knows more than any other Fallen,' said Orias. 'He seeks them out. He has crossed paths with hundreds, thousands of them. Sometimes alone, sometimes with allies, often recruiting as well as advising.'

'Cypher's interrogation will prove far more useful than yours,' said Anaziel.

'So you are going to be utterly dedicated to the hunt?' Luther looked at Orias with a sigh. 'I know the toll it can take.'

Humans were scattered across a whole world in small settlements that lacked anything but the most primitive means to communicate with each other, yet a single dominant principle remained: the hunt. It bound together the culture of Caliban across generations, dialect and geography. Outside of the Order, the ability to hunt and slay the Great Beasts was reserved for nobility, and from that power derived their authority and rights. Some were dutiful lords and ladies, others not so much, but any ruler that allowed the training of their knights to falter swiftly paid the price when a Great Beast entered their lands.

As well as these household forces, news of a Great Beast attracted any number of would-be knights seeking to complete their quest, and contingents of Wandered hoping to earn a wage. Trackers and guides, trappers and lure-mates all played their part, but tradition denied these commoners the right to kill a Great Beast.

Except for the Order, which cared nothing for bloodlines or name. For those not of high birth, entry was possible by squire-dom after proving oneself worthy to a knight of the Order, or by surviving the perilous journey to Aldurukh itself, a feat which thinned out all but the most courageous and intelli-gent low-born.

Technically I was a noble, the son of knights, but both my mother and father were of common stock. My father spoke little of his background and my mother respected his wishes, but taught me that she was the daughter of a cooper. They grew up together somewhere south and east of Aldurukh, so far away that its highest peak had been hidden beyond the horizon.

A Great Beast, one almost as fearsome as the Horn of Ruin, attacked their fort. Their ruler did not take her duties seriously and fled with her knights, abandoning those she should have protected. Most of the common folk resolved to stay in the castle though they had only ploughshares and fowl-hunting arms to protect themselves. My grandmother was not content with this, and with her children and several other families set off to seek protection from another lord.

Great were their trials, as can be imagined, but some of them survived the ordeals of the forest to make new homes in the foothills. Now teenagers, my mother and father decided that they would never again be reliant upon the faithless nobles, and when Sar Koralis and his troop passed through their settlement they learned of the Order. They ran away from their families and, as best they could, made their way into the mountains and eventually to the gates of Aldurukh itself.

I say this because it is important to know the beginnings of their knighthood to understand its end. They took seriously their vows to protect all others and they were always eager to join any expedition from Aldurukh, no matter how far afield it would take them, or for how long. The only time they spent more than a few months in the Angelicasta was during my mother's pregnancy and after my arrival. Even so, when I had been weaned off my mother's breast I was entrusted to the Order for my education both militant and moral, and my parents were as likely to be away on the hunt as at home to tend me. As it was said: blood shared between us is not as thick as blood spilled between us.

It is true to say that I probably had deeper feelings for my gain-parents than my birth family, for I spent more time with them of an age to appreciate the relationship. Even so, when I returned to Aldurukh and was accepted as a knight of the Order, I sought out my parents immediately so that they might know of my achievement, and they were proud of me. It was with the same eagerness that I put forward my name alongside theirs when next the Grand Master prepared a company for expedition into the forests.

These expeditions are not to be confused with the patrols that the Order conducted. Such routine ventures covered only the relatively small territory around Aldurukh, a cordon that ensured the safety of the Order and supported the neighbouring settlements. The patrols lasted many days, but the Order's mission was to quest across all of Caliban, to the furthest coasts, and even across the seas. Some expeditions lasted years, though the one to which I had committed myself was not so grand – perhaps six hundred kilometres west and south, to the area known simply as the Chasms.

Grand Master Dedrik died when I was but a youngster, and I have only vague recollection of the great funerary event that marked his internment into the Vaults of Thandor. Sarl Enneriel was slain by the Spiked Ironskin while I still lived away at Storrock. So I served Ocedon. He called me to his chambers alone, the night before we were due to leave.

Ocedon was short, perhaps one of the shortest knights I had known, but made up for that with broad shoulders and a barrel chest. Like those that came before, he was no administrator but a man of battlecraft and strategy. It was claimed that as a youth he had scandalised his noble family by seeking out manual labour – in the fields, hauling kegs, at the smithy bellows – so that he might build his body stronger than any man taller than him. He had sideburns that came nearly to his mouth but very little hair remained on his scalp, and his eyebrows were prominent enough that we younger knights joked they could still be seen poking through the closed visor of his helm. He was fierce in battle, a terror on the training ground, but softly spoken in private.

'You are warriors and ambassadors,' Grand Master Ocedon told me on the eve before our departure. 'With chainsword and bolt pistol you will slay the beasts of the forests. With your words you will spread the message of the Order.'

'What is the message of the Order?' I responded. Born in Aldurukh and having spent my life in its metaphorical shadow, the idea that the Order was not known the world over was alien to me.

'Equality and alliance,' Ocedon said.

We were sat by an electrical fire, one of only a few in Aldurukh, the buzz of its blue bars accompanying the clattering of plates as his companion, Sarl Fel, and half a dozen serfs readied the great table for our departure feast in the neighbouring hall.

I was not sure what to say so I simply nodded. The Grand Master frowned in reply.

'Do you understand what I mean with those words?' he asked me.

'I know what they mean to me, Sar Ocedon, but I cannot say what they mean to you,' I confessed.

His frown became a bemused smile.

'I am never quite sure whether you are clever, Sar Luther, or too clever,' he told me. There was wine in cups on a small table between us and he passed me one. 'You are by far the most remarkable knight the Order has seen for an age. Your natural skill with blade is equalled by your aptitude for diplomacy and mind for tactics. I have no fear in telling you this because I know that there is no arrogance in you, either.'

He leaned forward then, voice dropping conspiratorially.

'It is not for a Grand Master to name a successor, Luther, but should I persist for a few more years until you have more maturity, I cannot see how any other would replace me but you.'

It was quite the most remarkable endorsement I had heard and a great encouragement. I proved him right, years later, though my time as Grand Master was brief before we elevated the Lion to the new position of Supreme Grand Master. But the Lion was yet still a savage in the woods at that time and our paths would not cross for two more years, so I had no other measure of greatness than the man that had paid me these compliments.

'I am honoured that you regard me so highly, Sar Ocedon,' I told him, raising my wine in toast to him before taking a mouthful. 'I will do all I can to earn the trust and respect of the other masters so that, if they will it, your forecast becomes reality. But you did not explain to me what you mean by equality and alliance being the message of the Order.'

'Across Caliban, the nobles maintain control by dint of military power. Without the protection they offer, the common folk are vulnerable. Access to the best arms and armour, and the training to use them, is restricted to the knightly class, perpetuating their dominance. The Order does not arrange itself in this way, for we believe that every Calibanite has a *duty* to fight the Great Beasts, but also the *right* to do so. We offer a place to any man, woman or child that can prove themselves capable of that ideal.'

'That must make some of the nobles nervous,' I remarked, eliciting a nod from the Grand Master.

'It does indeed,' he said. 'But the Order is not so large, our recruits from the common folk not so many, that it really presents a threat to their power.'

'Yet the very idea that commoners can become knights is a notion they do not wish to encourage,' I persisted.

'Which is where the twin principle of alliance comes into it,' Ocedon told me, raising a hand with two split fingers as he made a point. He brought them together. 'The Order and the nobles fight beside each other. We enter their lands only by their permission. We pay for fodder and stabling. And, should any of their common folk voice discontent at their situation, we provide outlet for their dissatisfaction. Rather than foment insurrection in their homes, they can join us or set forth to Aldurukh to seek that life. In truth, very few question the roles they are born into and as many commoners are suspicious of the Order as the nobles. Some even believe we spirit away their sons and daughters and convert them into warriors! Peat burners, farmers, coopers, all the craft folk want to see their children succeed them or at least safe and well, not leaving on beast quests or slain on some distant castle wall.'

I had not considered this. Knighthood had been my preoccupation since I was old enough to conceive of my surroundings. The idea that others could seek contentment, even renown, in less martial pursuits was a revelation.

'Equal not just as individuals but also as cultures,' Ocedon continued, dropping his hand to his knee. 'The Order does not seek to replace the knightly class, but to work with them.

That is why we must ever be humble in our approach. It is not for us to sit in judgement of the world, nor to say how others must live. If others wish to emulate us, it will be because they are inspired not because they are cajoled. The moment that the nobles suspect the Order desires dominion, our cause is lost.'

I thought on these words until the banquet was announced, and then the merriment swiftly overtook me as I feasted with the nine other knights that would be setting out. As well as my parents, the expedition included three others more dear to me than most of my peers. Fyona, whom I had loved since adolescence. We were adults now and had spent years apart, but reunion had been sweet and our relationship was maturing. Then there was Maegon, who had come with me from Storrock. Last of that inner circle of companions was Sar Samael. He was a little older than I, and had been accepted into the Order during my absence, but we had swiftly become friends on our first patrol together.

The next day we headed out for the Chasms and for some it was the last time they set eyes upon Aldurukh.

The ride to the Chasms had event aplenty, such as would make a fine telling, but its conclusion is the point to which I must hasten while I can still distinguish memory from hallucination.

We were not the first to make the journey, and previous forays into the area had returned with the news that the principal ruler held court from Neortukh, the Peakgate. It had been years since that last contact and we did not know what welcome to expect as we came upon the broken landscape. The Chasms were so named for a combination of geological phenomena, being a range of high hills that had at some time in the past been rent by catastrophic movement, so that their valleys delved up to a kilometre below sea level. This instability continued, so that rarely a few years went past without some tumult in the depths that sent landslides tumbling and toppled watchtowers.

Despite this, or more accurately because of it, the Chasms were a prosperous region, with seams of precious ores open to minework and prospecting. The earthquakes also made no dissuasion to the flora or fauna of Caliban, and the steep slopes were as dangerous as any other stretch of forest. The knights of Peakgate were remarked afield for their decision to eschew mounts and fight on foot – a not unreasonable tactic given the terrain across which they held sway. This meant that they were also well versed in foraging and other wilderness skills, so that their patrols could cover the long, treacherous trails up and down the Chasms.

We made our presence known to a small outkeep within sight of the mound on which sat Peakgate, and the warden there informed us that the current lord was named Almanthis and would extend invitation to us without hesitation. He also revealed a wonder of Old Night known only to their knights – a communication device that could speak across the air.

A vox-caster! Not just one, of course, for there needs to be a receiver as well as a broadcast. The knights of Peakgate had sets of these in their scattered keeps so that they did not have to rely on sending couriers across the difficult valleys. To learn the ways of this ethereal communication would have been a great boon to the Order, and while the warden sent word by this means to Lord Almanthis, we agreed amongst ourselves that we should seek alliance with Peakgate if at all possible.

The warden's prediction was proven correct and within the hour he had received permission from his master to send us onward. A marvel to request orders and receive them in such a swift manner.

While our welcome was understated, it was nevertheless cordial and sincere. We met the lord and his advisors and soon made common ground – like Aldurukh, Peakgate was carved of the mountain itself, and we spent some time comparing our homes. The caverns of the Angelicasta were carved by nature's hand, but Peakgate's were the artifice of a far more mortal endeavour. As such the halls and chambers, once mine workings, were low of ceiling, and tended to the narrow as they had followed the ore veins. Electrical lighting, something of an extravagance in Aldurukh, was everywhere, and this answered my unspoken question of how the vox-casters – or longvoices as they called them – were continually powered. The mystery of this power network was something else I was keen to investigate.

We were feted and fed in the largest of the halls, close to the surface with natural windows along one wall where the sunlight blazed along shafts delved about three metres through the rock. Colourful banners were hung on the crudely excavated walls, and pillars of iron-reinforced wood held up the beams of the ceiling in places. It was very much a place of function adorned a little for the purposes of lordly aesthetic. It seemed to confirm the impression brought back by the previous expedition that the rulers and knights of Peakgate were not of very long noble lineage – commoners a few generations ago that had taken the mantle of lordship.

Though I was not the senior of our group, over our previous encounters with outsiders it had become clear that my tongue was the most accomplished, and so I took the lead in these introductions. After enquiring a little of the history of Peakgate, which the lord answered in vague terms, I spoke of the Order and our mission to seek out the beasts and slay them, and to protect any who trod the wilds of Caliban.

'What of foes of a different calibre?' one grey-haired courtier asked as she eyed us warily. 'The kind that walks on two legs?'

Almanthis seemed annoyed at the question, but when I enquired of him what his advisor meant he was forthcoming.

'Banditry, I must confess,' he told us, glaring at the woman.

'The forests to the west have become infested with outlaws that prey upon our mining caravans. They know the terrain too well to be caught, and their lairs are well protected. If we send more guards with the carts then we must reduce patrols elsewhere.'

'Surely you can just leave them to the forest and the Great Beasts?' suggested Sar Samael. 'In the wilds, no protection, it would just be a matter of time.'

'If that were true, they would already be dead,' grunted the old courtier.

'Indeed,' said Almanthis. 'It would seem they have a knack for survival, or some fortified lair.'

'Perhaps we could lighten the burden on your patrols while you conduct a campaign to dissuade these outlaws from remaining in your territory,' I suggested, but this was greeted with a chorus of disapproval from around the table.

'We cannot trust our defence to foreigners!' said one indignant noble, summarising the sudden mood.

Almanthis called for order but it took some time, as several arguments rippled through the council. When quiet was restored, the ruler of the Peakgate rubbed his chin and regarded us with a contemplative eye.

'It's not personal,' he assured us. 'Would the Order entrust its borders to others?'

'We do, as it happens,' replied my mother. 'Our security relies as much upon the cooperation of our neighbours as it does our own guard.'

'But we see your point,' I added quickly, trying to maintain what little favour we had been granted. I looked at my companions. 'Perhaps if we spread ourselves among the forces of the Chasms? A knight here or there would be no threat.'

This time the dissent was ours as my father shook his head and several of the others grumbled their objection.

'I would not have us scattered like chaff across a field,' my father insisted. As the most senior of us his will carried a lot of weight, and as a master he also had the authority of the Angelicasta. 'We come to hunt the Great Beasts, if permitted, and to offer the promise of future alliance.'

I would not be thwarted so easily and returned my attention to Almanthis.

'Perhaps, lord of Neortukh, there is a more specific task you could set us that would enable you to concentrate your efforts against these outlaws?'

'When you next heed word of a Great Beast, we could hunt it for you,' suggested Maegon. 'Surely you can trust us with such a mission?'

'And deny our squires a chance to earn their knighthood?' replied the same noble that had objected to us taking up the patrols.

'Even were that no consideration, you are novices in the Chasms,' said a dark-haired woman of middle age. I had barely noticed her before, but now that she drew attention to herself I realised I had paid her no mind because this was the first time she had spoken. There was an air of confidence about her and when she spoke, the others paid attention. 'Your destriers are unsuited to the terrain and you have no wildcraft in these lands. It is unfortunate, but equally unavoidable.'

'My daughter, Egrivere, Marchess of the Peaks,' the lord told us. 'She is right, and also you must understand that we have our own ways of meeting these challenges. Our knights are stationed across the territory in the waykeeps, ready to respond to our longvoices.'

'There is no great riding forth as you see from other realms, it simply is not practical to hunt every beast from the Peakgate,' Egrivere explained further, even as her look conveyed regret at this truth. 'Unless you happened to be close at hand, our foot knights would respond far more swiftly.'

Mention of the communications system renewed my desire to make some treaty with the Chasms and I spoke above my station.

'Then perhaps we can aid against the bandits?' I suggested, though I knew I would face objection from my own.

My offer brought swift censure from my father, by look if not by voice. He addressed his words to the lord of Peakgate.

'The Order is dedicated to the pursuit of the Great Beasts, but it appears that we can offer little to the people of the Chasms. You have our thanks for your hospitality and we would be grateful if you extend it another night. After that, we will occupy your counsel no more.'

'I am in accord,' announced Lord Almanthis. 'You are welcome to board at Peakgate for as long as you desire. There are any number of places within the town that would be grateful for your custom and your company. You may find yourselves harassed for news of wider goings-on, for very few folk make the effort to come to the Chasms.'

We took our leave of the council and headed from the lord's hall with an escort of local knights, to a hostelry they deemed suitable. The patron was indeed welcoming and inquisitive, but my father advised against mingling in the common room and instead we drank and dined in quarters to which we were billeted.

As we finished our meal I could hold my tongue no more.

'These longvoice devices are a miracle of the Lost Times,' I declared, pushing away my empty plate. 'If we could discover the secret of their creation, think of how much greater our reach would become. There are more wonders here too, for creating electricity, and maybe others we have not yet seen.'

'We are not here to increase our influence or to hoard archeotech, but to hunt the beasts of the forests,' Sar Gavriel replied, a sour-faced knight that I had disliked since our first meeting.

'We do not hunt bandits,' my father said.

I must confess that had he not been related to me, I might have resumed my silence then, but perhaps familiarity overcame due respect for a superior. Whatever the case, I banged my hand on the table in frustration, knocking over a glass.

'Stop being so short-sighted!' I snapped, and in the moment my temper took hold of me and I could not stop. 'You heard what their lord said. They can respond swiftly to any Great Beast, no matter where in their lands it arrives. Imagine that power in the hands of the Order. What if our allies in the neighbouring fortresses could signal for aid in moments and not days? What if our artisans could study this technology and make it portable? Our patrols might carry such a device on a wagon and report what they find as they move!'

'We are knights, not militia,' said Sar Gavriel. 'That means something to the Order. We hunt, we do not stand sentry.'

'Not quite so,' said my mother. 'The Order was founded to protect others.'

'They will not give us this technology,' my father said heavily. 'Not willingly. You see that they are distrustful. Why would they surrender this advantage to those they think may be enemies?'

'We come in alliance,' I insisted. 'If we prove to them our good intent, there is a chance. If we leave, there is none. What do we have to lose?'

What indeed? It seemed an easy decision to me, and I thought it the pride of the older knights that held them back, though I made no accusation openly.

'I cannot see how we can help,' said Fyona. 'Egrivere was right. We cannot chase our quarry up and down these valleys. Even if we did not become lost, or worse still led into ambush, what hope have we to succeed where the local knights have failed?'

She made a good point. What exactly could I offer that the knights of the Chasms did not possess?

'I cannot say,' I admitted. I looked at my father, offering conciliation. 'If I think of something, would you let me propose it to the lord? If we help Almanthis, imagine the good that can come of it.'

He was not an imaginative man, but he was also not an unfair one.

'We will leave in the morning unless you have something specific to offer to Almanthis.'

I nodded my thanks and agreement, made parting words with the others and retired, though I did not go to my chamber but decided to walk awhile to stir my creative thoughts. I almost bumped into a woman hurrying in through the door and she was likewise taken aback to see me. It was Egrivere.

'Sar Luther,' she exclaimed, a little more flustered than I thought the encounter warranted.

'Sarl Egrivere,' I replied, stepping back to allow her to enter. She stayed where she was.

'Marchess Egrivere,' she reminded me and I bowed in apology. 'I was seeking you, as a matter of fact.'

'Indeed? Well you have found me easily enough,' I replied.

'I have spoken with my father and he has granted leave for me to approach you,' she informed me quietly. 'I know that others on the council are suspicious of the Order, but I think there is much mutual gain in making league with one another.'

It was good to hear that someone among Almanthis' advisors was of like mind to myself. I wondered what precisely enticed her to the thought of alliance.

'I have just concluded similar negotiations with my own father,' I admitted with a smile. 'Perhaps we should conduct our conversation somewhere more comfortable than the threshold?'

We retired to a private room, sent for water and wine, and started to discuss how my company and I could be of service to the people of the Chasms. Between my tactical acumen and her local knowledge we finally devised a plan that might have merit, though it took us well past midnight. I returned to my chambers in sleepless mood, excited by the prospect of what we had decided.

The next day, Egrivere returned, this time with her lord and a few retainers. I had not had time to apprise my companions of the plan before their arrival and so they heard it for the first time also as they breakfasted.

'The concept is simple enough,' Egrivere began. 'The greatest advantage you bring is your speed over open ground. Your destriers can outpace any of our warriors.'

'Open ground is a rare commodity in the Chasms,' said Almanthis. 'It also comes with the disadvantage that our foes can see for a distance across it, giving them ample time to escape into less favourable terrain.'

'Which is why we must conceal ourselves from their view,' I countered. I looked to Egrivere and she nodded for me to continue. 'Surprise is essential and multiplies the impact of our speed.'

'And we must act swiftly, before word of the Order's presence is widely known,' added the marchess.

'I have had another thought on that,' I told her. 'The opposite is true. We must assume that the outlaws have eyes and ears in Peakgate. Sympathisers or paid agents. News of our arrival is wending its way across the Chasms as we sit here.'

'Then our enemies will be keen to track your movements and our plan cannot work,' said Egrivere, her expression glum.

'Quite the opposite!' I told her and the others. 'Our small company will make great show of leaving Peakgate and the Chasms. Word will spread that we found no welcome here, but I am sure you have some means by which we might return in secret.'

'It can be arranged,' said Almanthis.

'You have said nothing of what you intend us to do,' complained my father. 'What plan have you concocted?'

Egrivere and I looked at each, to see which of us would answer. I nodded for her to explain.

'The ore wagons from the mines are large, each certainly able to conceal two of your knights,' she said, looking at my companions. 'They come to Peakgate to unload their cargoes, travelling along the only road we can maintain – the causeway deep. In return, payment is sent to the mines but we do not say when. We will, by roundabout means, allow the rumour to spread that the next caravan will include the payment chest.'

'And just hope the brigands attack?' said Fyona.

'We will make the prize irresistible,' I said to her. 'A particularly bountiful reward for striking a new seam. Of course, to maintain secrecy, there will be no additional guards.'

'The road is long, the forest and ravines close at times,' said Almanthis. 'How can you know when the outlaws will attack?'

'One of the wagons will break a wheel near the ford over the Steepwater. If the brigands have been paying attention, they will seize the opportunity. The area either side of the ford is flat for nearly close to a kilometre, but it will be a lure too tempting, I think.'

There were other questions, but Egrivere and I had been diligent and were able to address any concern or argument. I could tell that my father and the older knights were not keen, but they kept their reservations silent in front of the local contingent.

It took some time, but both parties agreed to the plan and it was decided to enact it immediately. I was pleased that I had managed to convince both my peers and our new allies to work together, and must admit I thought myself quite clever for doing so and overlooked Egrivere's contributions when I looked back in later life.

The lord and his retainers made a show of leaving the hostelry in some ill temper, and we followed after in short order, talking loudly amongst ourselves about the poor reception we had received in Peakgate. We rode from the town gate and continued for a day, into the forests south of the fortress.

That night a rider came to us and guided us to caves that linked to a watchtower close to the road, and by this means were we able to ensconce ourselves upon the wagons two days later.

It was an uncomfortable journey for us and our steeds, rocked and jostled along the winding road, resting as best we could amid fodder sacks and our belongings. I rode with Fyona and we spent the time as well we could, but the very close proximity of two equine onlookers and the necessity of keeping on our armour quashed any amorous intentions we might have harboured.

On the third day out, the shouts of the small guard contingent warned us that the decoy wagon had thrown its wheel. We heard splashing and realised that our driver had continued on a little way into the ford itself.

We waited expectantly, weapons at the ready, patting our destriers to keep them quiet. A few minutes passed and then we heard the sharp, distinctive report of a rifle. Warning cries sounded around us and more gunfire followed. The local knights, four of them, had been ordered to take cover and protect themselves after a brief show of defiance. We worked the toggles that held down the back of the heavy cover and freed the bolts of the tailgate so that it would fall easily.

Still we did not reveal ourselves. I tried to picture the scene by combining what I knew of our surrounds from my conversation with Egrivere with the sounds around us. The valley flattened for just shy of two kilometres with the ford pretty much dead centre, as if at the bottom of a shallow bowl, almost completely ringed by the forest edge. The floor of the hollow was a water meadow, soft underfoot but passable, but too wet for trees to take root, leaving it open but for a few scattered thickets. It would be heavy for the destriers too, but over the distance I thought them speedier than a man or woman on foot.

The brigands had to break cover and come to the caravan before we could act, otherwise they would be able to reach the safety of the trees again before we overtook them. The closer they came, the better our chances of the counter-attack succeeding, but we dared not even twitch a wagon cover for fear of betraying our presence. We were wholly reliant upon those outside the wagons to pick the best moment.

The drivers called their surrenders after a couple of minutes of sporadic gunfire. We heard the thud of feet on the boards followed by a splash as ours abandoned her place behind the train of sturdy ponies.

One hand on the saddle bow, the reins in the other, I stood next to Accadis while Fyona readied to mount her destrier behind me. A minute passed, then another. I forced myself to breathe steadily and resisted the urge to check my pistol was loose in its holster. I could imagine the brigands closing on their prize.

Suddenly a horn sounded, clear and long.

I hauled myself onto Accadis' back even as she sprang forward, knowing the call to action had been sounded. We bounded from the back of the wagon first, Fyona just moments behind, to plunge into the shallow water. Foam sprayed around me as Accadis surged back towards the bank.

Ahead I could see the others galloping along the road. Around two dozen men and women on foot, about sixty or seventy metres away, were fleeing up the grassy slope towards the treeline, the snap of bolts following them. A few turned to shoot back with crude arquebuses, their fire hurried and poorly aimed. I dragged out my chainsword but did not ignite the motor – instead I readied to use the flat of it like a club, to take at least one of the fleeing brigands alive. If we could learn where they made their lair it would earn even more favour from Lord Almanthis.

I steered Accadis out of the river and up the slope, galloping hard after a man and woman in padded jerkins over ragged smocks. The man glanced back and saw me closing on them. Urging his companion onwards, he turned and pulled a long pistol from his belt.

I saw the flare of powder and puff of smoke a split second before I heard the crack of firing and the clang of the bullet hitting the chamfron across Accadis' chest. The destrier carried on without pause while the man broke open the chamber of his pistol and pushed a fresh projectile into the breech.

Too late he raised the weapon again. Accadis rode into him, just a glancing blow with her shoulder but enough to throw him to the ground with a cry of pain. I kicked her onwards, after the woman, bringing the inert chainsword back. In three more powerful strides my steed brought me alongside and I swung, my blow connecting with the back of the woman's shoulder, sending her sprawling into the long grass.

Accadis circled as I swapped chainsword for pistol.

'Hold!' I called to both of them, moving my aim from the woman to the man. 'Disarm yourselves!'

He opened fire but the bullet whined some way past my right shoulder. I held my finger from the trigger and called again for him to put down the weapon, moving my aim to the woman pushing to her feet a few metres from me. With his companion under threat he complied, tossing the empty pistol aside.

I risked a glance along the slope and saw that Fyona was in pursuit of three others along the riverbank, her pistol barking loud. In the other direction, knights of the Order were engaged in herding a couple of surrendered outlaws towards the caravan while others were riding down those that had almost reached the cover of the treeline. The buzz of chainswords preceded cries of panic and pain.

About forty metres away stood a riderless destrier. I could see the gleam of armour in the grass but could not tell who had fallen or if they still lived. Searching the other knights, I could not tell who was who at this distance.

'Back to the wagons,' I called to my prisoners and they moved down the slope at my command.

A few minutes later the echoes of the last bolt detonation faded away. Six outlaws had surrendered and we kept watch over them close to the wagons. Their brigandage obviously was not very successful for their clothes were little more than rags, and such weapons as we had confiscated in poor repair. They seemed on the verge of starvation.

Garrig, senior of the Peakgate knights, approached with his small troop, fusils at the ready.

'What did you spare them for?' he asked, waving his weapon towards the prisoners. 'The lord has ordered the execution of any man or woman that raises arms against him.'

'Your master can kiss my scabby arse!' one of the captive women shouted. 'He's no lord here!'

'Hold!' my father demanded, moving his steed to block Garrig as he raised his gun towards the prisoners. 'Steady your temper and we might yet find out where more of your enemies are to be found.'

'They'll tell us nothing,' the guard commander insisted, but he stepped back with weapon lowered all the same.

'Where is your camp?' I asked the man who had shot at me.

'Camp?' he laughed back, bitterness written in his features. 'Do we look like we have a camp? Or even a tent?'

'Almanthis' soldiers harry us from valley to valley,' said another. 'But it was the Cragshadow that drove us out in the first place.'

'Cragshadow?' said Maegon. 'What is that?'

'A myth,' claimed Garrig with a snort. 'An excuse made up by work-shy commoners. Thieving cavefolk!'

He tried to come forward again but my father guided his steed to intercept him.

'Explain yourself,' he said to Garrig.

'I don't answer to you, foreigner,' the man replied with a sour expression. 'Just remember who you're working for.'

'I work for nobody,' my father told him. 'I am a knight of the Order and accept only the authority of the Grand Master.'

'Well, you're in the Chasms now, knight of the Order, and these are Almanthis' lands.' The other guards did not share their leader's belligerence, hanging back from the confrontation.

'In name only,' said one of the prisoners, a skinny man no older than I, a cut on his brow where he had fallen. 'We sent for help against the Cragshadow and what did we get? Demands for even more ore. He is a slavemaster not a noble!'

'Jumped up ore-digger, no better than us,' added another prisoner.

'You'll pay for that,' said Garrig and brought up his fusil. From the saddle, my father kicked the weapon aside and pulled out his bolt pistol. The other guards raised their weapons hesitantly, their gazes moving from my father to Garrig, unsure what to do.

'You are four against ten,' my mother said quietly, resting her hand on the grip of the pistol at her saddle. 'Make your next words soft and your actions slow.'

Garrig fumed but said nothing, eventually lowering his weapon.

'The Cragshadow is a Great Beast?' I said to the woman I had captured.

'It's a lie!' yapped Garrig. 'There's no creature made of rock that can move from shadow to shadow.'

'It haunts the mines to the north,' the woman told me, scowling at the guard. 'It comes from the depths at night and preys upon the sleeping. We tried to fight it but had to flee. We daren't go back in the mines and it ranges further and further from its lair.'

I could see my father's thoughts as clearly as I might trace the words on a page. It did not matter that we had an agreement with Lord Almanthis, the hunt took precedence. I also knew that there would be no argument against him in this matter.

'Show us,' he said to the woman. 'Take us to the monster and we will slay it.'

There was further protest from Garrig and suspicion from the outlaws, but we mustered our belongings.

'You either lead us to this creature, or we look for it ourselves and leave you with them,' I said quietly, indicating the Peakgate knights with a glance.

The prisoners soon voiced their desire to show us the location of the beast that had caused their woes.

'The lord will have you driven out of the Chasms for this, if he doesn't take your heads for consorting with outlaws!' Garrig threatened, but we knew his words were empty. As much as some folk did not welcome the Order, most knew that to raise arms against one of our knights was to invite terrible retribution from Aldurukh.

Even so, my father was riding a narrow line between his oaths as a knight to hunt the Great Beasts and the needs of diplomacy. I tried one last attempt to salvage something of value for the Order.

'I thought you were knights?' I exclaimed to Garrig and his warriors. 'Protectors of the Chasms, brave sons and daughters of Peakgate. A Great Beast has been sighted. The call to arms has been made. Which of you refuses the quest?'

'Risk our lives for these outlaws?' said Garrig.

'No, you risk yourselves for the glory of the hunt,' I argued. 'The Great Beasts care not for our laws when they feast on the flesh of those we swore to protect. Brigand, commoner, noble.

It matters nothing. Earn your arms and show your families why they should be proud of you. Or would you have the story told in Peakgate that a band of outsiders were braver than the knights of the Chasms?'

Not my most original oratory but it worked all the same. The other three knights called Garrig to them and they held quick conference. Garrig returned and, to his credit, he seemed genuinely shamed by my words.

'These are our lands,' he announced. 'Nobody says the knights of Peakgate are cowards.'

So it was decided that we would all go in search of the Cragshadow, whether to slay it or prove it false. It was not the most promising stage of our fledgling relationship with the Chasms, but at least I had averted outright antipathy. It was my hope that by fighting together we might demonstrate to Almanthis the benefits of future cooperation.

Hopes and expectations can change swiftly, though. By the time midnight arrived, alliance with Peakgate was the least of our concerns.

My brother-in-arms Sar Omeniel died first.

The land about the mine entrance was a mess of spoil dumped over generations, such that even the forest did not come within a hundred metres of the cavern. No light reached the bottom of the canyon, so we had advanced over the broken heaps with saddle lamps on, our weapons at the ready.

We had thought any attack would come from the blackness of the mine, but with a screech like a tortured owl the Cragshadow swooped upon us from behind, ripping Omeniel from his steed. Blood splashed across Maegon beside me, spattering her lamp so that the light threw ovals of darkness ahead.

The thud of Omeniel's body drew us to the left, bolt pistols and fusils lifted skyward.

'You never said the bastard thing could fly!' yelled Garrig, addressing the gaggle of prisoners surrounded by our short column.

'Above us,' Fyona warned, tracking her pistol ahead as she heard something in the darkness. 'It lifted Omeniel without effort.'

'Something that big should not be that fast,' said my mother.

'It's made of darkness, born of the shadows,' wailed one of the outlaws. I could see that he was going to flee.

'Stay with us if you want to live,' I barked.

He did not listen and broke from the group, darting behind Accadis. I turned in the saddle to see him sprint across the beam from Maegon's lamp before disappearing. A few seconds later we heard the flap of gigantic wings and a scream from the night.

The foot knights had their own light, a bright blue lantern held on a pole, and clustered beneath it like eggs in a nest, fusils presented in a small thicket. They were slowly retreating away from the mine, stepping together in drilled fashion.

'Hold your positions!' bellowed my father, noting their manoeuvre was taking them further from us. 'We fight together.'

'We're not dying for some filthy outlaws,' Garrig called back. 'We'll come back in the daytime with a full force and burn the thing out.'

We formed a living corral around the former miners, using our destriers as a barricade, our lamps shining outwards across the broken ground of the spoil heaps, pieces of ore and discarded tools glittering in the glare. Omeniel's mare stood atop a nearby mound, eyes rolling, head moving from side to side as she sought the creature that had taken her rider.

'Widen cordon,' my father commanded, voice calm but carrying across the thud of my heart. His ease settled my nerves and I urged Accadis forward a few steps, eyes trying to pierce the dark outside the cone of light, finger on the trigger of my pistol.

A sudden downdraught announced the Cragshadow's arrival. I thought I spied a darkness briefly eclipse the sliver of stars high above the valley. A second later, a terrible slashing of flesh and crunching of bone sounded behind me. The captives screamed in horror, one of them uttering a drawn-out shriek of pain. Twisting in the saddle I saw only movement against the pale spoil, a thrashing darkness from which erupted a trio of running people. I saw a reflection in a plate-sized eye as Fyona heeled her mount around, bringing the beam of her lamp to bear.

The Cragshadow exploded upwards in a flap of wings, leaving only the impression of a vast black shape. Body parts rained down in its wake, bouncing across the scree and slag.

'It shuns the light!' cried Sar Gavriel, reining his destrier to the left, sweeping the saddle lamp across the fleeing prisoners. 'Stay in the light!'

A couple of them stumbled to a terrified standstill, clutching at each other. The third disappeared, heading back the way we had entered. For a few dozen metres he was illuminated by the lamp of the foot knights. The warriors of Peakgate fired a salvo of shots at the fleeing commoner, sending him scurrying into the night gloom. His shrieks followed soon after, accompanied by loud snapping and the scratch of monstrous claws on stone.

The foot knights continued on, creating a pool of light that moved slowly along the valley. Their pace was not swift but it was steady and soon we were separated by fifty metres and more, two distinct circles of sanctuary light.

'What are you doing?' my mother demanded, moving across the gap they had opened between us. 'These are your people. You swore to protect them!'

'Outlaws!' Garrig yelled back. His fusil shook in his grasp; the gleam of its powercell underlit his face, exaggerating his fearful expression. 'They gave up that protection when they

LUTHER: FIRST OF THE FALLEN 173

refused the lord. They brought this on themselves, digging too deep, getting greedy.'

'You will never make it out of here,' I shouted to them. 'This beast is not going to be afraid of your light for much longer.'

'Nor ours,' said Maegon. 'We must find some way to kill it.'

'We need more light,' said Sar Samael. He rode over to the two last captives. It was the man and woman I had taken prisoner. 'You must have lamps for the mines.'

'It broke them all when it first attacked,' said the woman. 'Those with lamps it killed before the others.'

'Garrig is right, we unleashed this nightmare,' moaned the man. 'Broke into its lair in the deeps.'

'There are tracking flares and blasting charges,' the woman said hurriedly, thrusting a finger towards the mine entrance. 'The depot, behind that wall to the left.'

At the very limit of our lamps I could see a wall about chest-high, and beyond it a structure of heavy beams.

'Blasting charges, you say?' said my father.

Just then a shadowy thunderbolt crashed into Sar Samael. His destrier screamed as sabre-claws sank into its flank, bowling it over, even as bloodstained jaws closed around Samael's arm.

I opened fire, the flicker of my bolts chasing the Cragshadow up into the darkness. There was no thump of secondary detonation. I had either missed or the warhead had not penetrated its hide.

'Cover each other with your lamps,' my mother called out, riding back to us. 'Give it no prey unlit.'

We managed to arrange ourselves in a ring, illuminating one another with our lamps, while the two outlaws stuck close to my father, avoiding the shadow cast by his mount.

I had always thought some of the more complex drills we had trained and paraded as aesthetic rather than useful. That changed as we moved as a group towards the depot wall, some of us riding sideways or even backwards to maintain the ring of light. Looking back along the valley I could see the glimmer of the foot knights nearly half a kilometre away.

Of the Cragshadow there was no sign. No noise of eating, no beat of wing, no silhouette against the night sky.

'What is your intent?' Sar Gavriel asked my father.

'We will lure it down and slay it with explosives,' he replied. 'It seems the only way to be sure.'

It must have been half an hour until we were within a dozen metres of the depot wall. The gate was at the far end, closest to the mine entrance, and we could see the heavy chains about the lock.

'I suppose you did not think to bring a key?' my father said to the captives. It was not often he showed humour, and I realised that he was as scared as I was but had hidden it so well he appeared uncaring.

At that moment we heard distant cries from along the valley. The smudge of light that was the foot knights wavered, and I could imagine the lantern pole swaying violently. Then all went dark.

'The cowards are dead,' said Maegon.

'And the beast is overcoming its distaste for the light,' I added with some misgivings.

My father was swifter than I was on the implications of this.

'We must act now, while it is still yonder,' he snapped, spurring his steed forward, breaking the ring. He rode up to the depot gate and fired his pistol twice, shattering the lock. Rearing, his destrier kicked open the heavy wooden gate and they disappeared within.

'It is coming back!' yelled Sar Samael, whose lamp happened to be the one directed down the valley. 'I saw it taking off.'

'Rodiel!' My mother called my father's name, riding towards the gate. 'Rodiel, come back!'

Samael opened fire and the second of his shots blossomed against something about a hundred metres away. Maegon, Fyona, Gavriel and I added our own bolts, a fusillade that lit the air with ascending sparks. Another detonation, seventy metres distant.

I spared a glance over the wall and saw that my father was at the storehouse door, dismounted. I heard the rev of his chainsword as he prepared to cut through the wood.

'Hurry!' I yelled to him. 'Hurry up!'

But I could see that he would not be swift enough. The Cragshadow was closing fast, skimming just above the light of our lamps, the tips of immense wings dipping into and out of view.

'Over here!' shouted my mother, firing her pistol. 'Over here, you foulspawn!'

She kicked into the flanks of her steed and broke away, plunging into the dark, still firing. By the flash of bolt propellant we traced her progress towards the mine entrance. Above, the broad shadow of the Great Beast altered as it turned, swinging almost directly over me as it switched its attention to the prey in the darkness.

'Shoot it!' I cried, though no command was needed. We emptied the magazines of our pistols towards the Cragshadow, but to no avail.

My last sight of my mother was of her standing up in the stirrups, the flash of a bolt detonation illuminating her and the open, dragon-like maw of the Cragshadow. An image burned into my memory like a brand mark.

I heard the clatter of armour and screech of tearing metal, and yelled wordlessly, pulling the trigger again and again though my pistol was empty.

It was Sar Gavriel's voice that cut through my shock.

'It is coming back for your father, Luther. Reload!'

I acted on instinct, pulling fresh ammunition from my saddlebag, even as the winged shape of our foe swooped around towards us.

'It's hurt!' Maegon called, and I could see she was right. The rise and fall of its wings was more laboured, and it seemed to favour its left side. Unfortunately, it also seemed to have fully overcome its distaste for light, either through desperation or rage, and came straight for us into the beams.

Accadis saved my life, throwing herself sideways to the ground just as a sweeping claw cleaved the space where we had been. Sar Samael was not so fortunate: the other foot snapped around his helm and ripped his head free, the decapitated corpse falling sideways in the saddle as his terrified destrier bolted.

The monster passed over the depot wall to where my father stood at the open door of the storehouse. Rather than flee inside, my father charged the Great Beast, chainsword flashing towards its face. It veered away from the screaming teeth of the motorised blade, skidding into the ground, pinning my father beneath its bulk as the two of them crashed into the wall of the storehouse.

Accadis stood with me still clinging to the saddle, and I watched as my father hacked at his enemy's throat from below. As it tried to pull itself up, disentangling its wings, he dropped his chainsword and wrapped an arm around its lower jaw, pulling it down. I could not fathom his intent, except to use his weight to prevent it from taking flight again. Unnatural muscle strained against servos, the Cragshadow snarling, my father's armour whining mechanically.

With his other hand my father fired a bolt into the storehouse.

Explosions blossomed upwards for what felt like minutes, though was likely only a few seconds. Fire of red and blue engulfed the beast and my father, shredding wings, burning flesh to bone, turning armour to molten bullets. The blast wave sent charred timber flying, passing over the wall to flatten steeds and riders.

* * *

Anaziel and Orias stared at Luther in rapt silence, two giant statues.

'Ears ringing, we surveyed the scene,' he told them. 'The Cragshadow was dead, my father and mother with it. That is always the price of the hunt – death. Often the prey, but sometimes the hunter.'

'What happened to the outlaws?' asked Orias. 'Did they make peace with Lord Almanthis?'

'There were no outlaws, not really,' Luther replied. 'Just miners that had stood up to him. We only saved the two of them, but it went poorly for us all the same. Almanthis was shamed, both for his treatment of his people and for refusing to ride out against the Cragshadow. The Order was banned from the Chasms, and it was not until the rise of the Lion that we went back. After hearing of our campaign against the beasts, Egrivere overthrew her father and swore Peakgate to our goals.'

'Not the worst of outcomes,' said Orias. 'For one that condemned millions to death, you seem squeamish about sacrifice.'

'Death does not unsettle me,' Luther growled. 'All things except perhaps the Lion and the Emperor die eventually. But the hunt… the hunt was service to Death. When the Lion proposed that we exterminate the Great Beasts forever, he saw it as a way of taming Caliban. I thought of it as a way of uniting the knightdoms. Equality and alliance, the soul of the Order. What goal does your hunt really serve?'

Orias looked Luther in the eye without flinching.

'Salvation,' he said.

'Salvation?' Luther laughed, and in releasing his humour was gripped by an overwhelming mania. 'Salvation? You cannot be saved! How can you be saved from yourselves? There is nobody to forgive you. Nobody to forgive me. There is nothing, no salvation, no hope, no respite.'

Disgust twisted the faces of the two Space Marines as Luther continued to rant. He saw in them the hatred of the Lion burning again, as he had seen it in the face of his gain-brother as the walls of Aldurukh crumbled beneath them, locked together in death. In remembering the fall of Aldurukh he tried to recall what he had been doing when the Lion had found him. He could think of nothing beyond the glare of his gain-brother.

He was a fool for thinking he would find forgiveness there.

'We are all damned!' he shouted at the Dark Angels. 'No son of Caliban will ever escape the shadows cast by old treacheries. The galaxy burns and we should perish with it. Death will not absolve us, our sin is eternal!'

The Space Marines withdrew and in the moments before stasis returned, visions of the Angelicasta aflame breached the mind of the oracle. Whether from the past or the future, Luther could not tell.

TALE OF THE TRAITOR

Orias returned several more times, in what felt like a short period, presumably before he departed to lead his newly founded Chapter. Tatraziel did not return and in his last visit Orias told Luther that the Dark Oracle, as he was now known, was unlikely to be visited again. His usefulness had waned.

With only the vaguest sense of time passing while in stasis, Luther fell back into lengthy hallucinations, a living dream of bloodshed and death. He tried to seize hold of what he saw, to secure it in his memory so that he might relate it once more to his interrogators, but every scene slipped away in the end, forced out by fresh visions or drowned by a resurgence of distant memories.

Despite Orias' warning, a Supreme Grand Master came again, though more than a millennium had passed since Luther's last interrogation.

He spent much of his time spouting fragments of his visions, warning of warriors in green that would darken a star and metal-fanged beasts that rode the winds of a distant world.

Looking at the Space Marine commander that visited the cell, Luther could barely see him, a shadow of secrecy and death swathing his form.

'Death clings like a shroud to your armour, fake knight,' rasped the former Grand Master. 'You have become the shadow you seek, and your own doom is the sword in your hand. He that summons the storm is not immune to its lightning. You cannot ride the thunder, it will deafen you to the pleas of your victims.'

The Dark Angel did not take kindly to this and did not return, but another replaced him after more stasis nightmares, more alike to the Lion than Luther had seen for some time. Hair of gold hung to the warrior's shoulders and his armour was dark green with heraldry of red and white, the symbol of the Deathwing prominent on his pauldron. There was much gold decoration, his chestplate embossed with the face of a roaring lion, and his face was heavy with creases of age. A golden aura surrounded him and it took some time before Luther realised it was a projection in reality and not some imagining of his fevered mind.

The man spoke a name: Nahariel, and demanded to know if Luther or the Order had ever visited an area called the Veiled Region.

'I see a veil lifted, a curtain of fire that leaves bright purity in its wake,' replied Luther, speaking even as the vision came to him. 'Star systems, a hundred stars, a hundred stars dying as you watch. The darkness falling again. I see an angel of black, shrouded in mists. It is his voice. His words are the fog, clouding him from scrutiny.'

'A sorcerer?' asked Nahariel. 'Some kind of mind-controlling powers?'

Luther stared at the Space Marine, aware of his presence again. He swallowed and took a deep breath. The room started to solidify, the walls thickening against the backdrop of stars, the floor chill under bare feet.

'He needs no sorcery. His words are spring rain on seeds that have seen drought for an age. What he says does not matter, only the way he says it. He gives hope to the hopeless. He speaks of victory rather than sacrifice. He promises reward over service.'

'Falsehoods,' spat Nahariel. 'A deceit to sway the weak and ignorant.'

'Oh yes, very much so,' said Luther with a smile. He felt anchored, for a time at least. His stomach grumbled in hunger and his throat was dry with thirst. 'I have spun words in many ways, to say the same thing in a dozen different guises to a dozen different audiences, but I sense this preacher has a gift.'

'A preacher? So, our subverter comes from the priesthood!'

'There is nothing holy, it is just a raiment he chooses to wear. His soul is garbed in lies but the downtrodden, the forgotten, listen to him. They know that he cannot deliver what he promises but they choose to believe, to blindly wish for a solution to a problem that is beyond their power.' Luther saw a flash of gunfire, a body falling. He thought he recognised the face for a fleeting instant but could not believe what he saw. A screaming mob filled his ears with their shouting and stamping, his view obscured by countless faces twisted in hate. He stared hard at Nahariel. 'Few people wish to know the truth about the universe. We each just choose the set of lies that comforts us most. You think I am a traitor, but I have never wronged you. You quest for vengeance of a memory... No, less than a memory. The legend of a memory that another once had.'

'The Rock is all that remains of Caliban, proof enough of your betrayal, Luther.'

'It was not my guns that broke the world, Nahariel. The Lion chose to shatter his planet rather than see it lost another way. A brave choice, one that I forced upon him. But you never set foot on Caliban.' The last moments of Caliban's life flashed through Luther again. A world fragmenting, the storm of the warp tearing it apart even as unnatural forces exploded within his thoughts. He became agitated at the recollection and started to pace, fingers fidgeting. 'It was *my* home! You were not born there. Even the Lion was not born there, though it was the bosom that raised him and received nothing but pillaging in return. You call me guilty of this crime, but cannot bring a single victim as witness! Only I know what happened.'

He folded into a sullen silence, crouching, head buried in his hands.

'Alldric the Subverter,' said Nahariel. 'The false preacher. Demagogue of a Hundred Worlds. You spoke before, a long time ago, of a hundred stars dying.'

'Do you never learn?' groaned Luther, not looking up. 'Kill Alldric, take him prisoner and make him repent, throw his body parts to the masses. It never changes anything. You cannot turn blind worship and hate of the unknown into a force for creation. Survival is never an inspiration, only desperation. And the Emperor cannot promise anything better. Your kind, the Space Marines, the warlords, tore up the last chance for humanity.'

'There are some of us that continue to fight for that future even if it seems too distant to hope for,' said Nahariel. 'Only sacrifice, unflinching duty and resolute defiance of our foes can deliver anything. And it is my duty to find the Fallen sowing strife along the Veiled Regions and bring him to the Rock so that he can repent.'

'And what then?' Luther looked at the commander between splayed fingers. 'Removing a falsehood does not create truth. When Alldric is gone, who will the people turn to?'

Nahariel said nothing. Luther fell forward onto his knees and ran a hand through his sweat-thick hair. Sitting back on his haunches he looked at Nahariel with a haunted gaze.

* * *

There have always been those that listened to our wishes and confessions. From long before the birth of the Imperium, entities far older than the Emperor Himself have offered mortals the means to realise their dreams. In the books from the Lupus library I read about these otherworldly powers. In the tomes given to me by Erebus I learned more of their nature and the realm of the warp.

The most obvious lesson was that there were no obvious lessons. Any power, any knowledge worth gaining is achieved through the equal payment of effort and will. Those that had transcribed the words I read had done so upon the efforts of others, just as I stood upon their shoulders to see further. And among all of the stories of gods and nephilla, souls and sorcery, there was hidden a far more elusive but valuable truth.

Ironically, I learned that there is no truth.

The stars care nothing for truth. Whether these words are true or not will alter the orbits of worlds by no margin at all. Great leaders speak of seeking our true potential. Priests speak of higher truths. Philosophers quest for inner truths.

None of them will find what they are looking for, because it does not exist: not in here nor out there, nor even in the beyond of the warp.

The key to balancing this dichotomy is held in your thoughts. The warp. The reflection of us that we choose not to see. The Soulsea, the Fire of Creation, the Abyss of the End. It is us and we are it. Our emotions become energy, given direction and form of a kind. So it is that when we listen to the whispers of the warp, it is not some predatory deity lusting after our spirit. It is ourselves, telling us what we wish to hear. The secrets we keep from our conscious minds, the desires we dare not admit to ourselves.

The truth of temptation by the powers of the warp is that there is no temptation. It is not an external thing. They do not create desire in us, any more than a fire can make fuel for itself. When we battle it is for our own designs. When we fear it is for our lives and those around us. When we hope it is to better the course of our existence. When we lust it is for the things we have always wanted.

These feelings are not placed into us by evil beings.

Let me tell you about corruption, for I can swear there is no other soul in this universe that has seen it the same way as these eyes. From within. And yet now I have been freed.

Haven't I?

Maybe not. Maybe even this story is a part of the lies woven by my deeds. I cannot tell for I am within it, and no other can gainsay me for they have not lived the life I have. There is but one witness and it is a narrator most unreliable.

That is the universal truth of Chaos. Yes, Chaos. The force of the warp that has many names, all of them forbidden on the lips of man and woman. It does not corrupt. We corrupt ourselves in its service. That is why we cannot speak of it.

To know is to be tempted.

If I put a gun in your hand and tell you not to use it, to fire one shot is to be damned forever, and then release an Anterion tiger into the room, who is to blame for your downfall? Me, or you? Maybe the tiger, though it also cannot be other than what it is.

The other great lie we tell ourselves on that downward path is that we are different. We did not take the shortcuts others did. We did not use Chaos instead of sacrifice, for we have studied hard and given up much to learn what we have learned.

But we have erred in that reasoning. The lie has taken root well into our thoughts because we cannot admit our own corruption. We have chosen to avoid death, to avoid defeat, to avoid deprivation or despair. Whatever caused us to indulge our temptation, we could have endured it. We could have *failed* and allowed the cruel tides of fate to wash away our lives without leaving a mark.

Yet we gave in. We thought we deserved better. There was a way to make fate our steed, to ride the tides where we wished.

The biggest lie is thinking that any of us are different.

Fools, chaining ourselves to a lightning strike in the hope its bolt would land where we desired but never really in control of its course. The lie grows. The cause is good, selfless, noble even. Yet the greatest man or woman of charity takes satisfaction from their deeds. Even the martyr glories in the moment of demise, having been proven righteous. The truth we deny is that every act is a selfish act, so why not embrace it? Why meander through the mud of poor fortune that befouls other mortals? Why be mortal at all, doomed to die and see our legacies eventually crumble to nothing?

I travelled that road for years. Sometimes slowly, other times with rash haste. I see it behind me, linking me still to those events that have led to this day and this speech. Like all successes and failures, through the selfish lens, it seems inevitable. I was trapped because of the failings of others.

No. It was my weakness that carried me here, and in owning that I am free of the corruption.

Are there times we can step off the path? Yes. Yes there are. Opportunities to see past the illusion of external truth and witness ourselves. We are truth, we decide what is real and what is a lie. A few manage to seize that moment, and probably never realise how close they came to damnation. A clarity of thought, a neuron firing that creates a moment of humility. Even the unseen decision to take a step left rather than right, into the course of bolt or bullet.

I think I am the only one that has travelled the road almost to its end, to have savoured its power and yet rejected it. And I think I only managed that because I had practised, unknowingly.

When the final decision came to me, I could see it clear, for events had seen fit to give me rehearsal.

It was at Zaramund. Of course it was.

Having taken possession of a sizeable transport fleet, my confinement on Caliban was brought to an end. That decision itself was no easy one, for though I had been working for Caliban's independence, the acquisition of ships and breaking of my banishment was a direct act against the will of the Lion. There were no speeches that could make it seem otherwise. All that took part in the endeavour knew we were now rebels, opposed to the rule of the Lion.

We had but one warship, and that was a matter that needed swift addressing, for a transport is only of use if it reaches its target. Thirty thousand knights of the Order, Space Marines one and all, was an army worthy of any commander, but they were worthless if they were blown up in the void.

Terrible storms had swept through the galaxy, heralding the Warmaster's own steps on a path of damnation parallel to mine. Our Navigators could see the beacons at Zaramund well enough though, and the taking of a shipyard seemed like the perfect first test for our fledgling force. As it was an important juncture to and from Terra, possession of Zaramund would be a bargaining point in its own right, and it would see us able to spread our influence far.

It transpired that Zaramund was no military test. It was beset by factions like many other systems in the galaxy: some for Horus, others loyal to the Emperor. The arrival of a sizeable force of Dark Angels, for we travelled in the cloak of the First Legion, soon quelled all dissent.

In the absence of leadership there will always be a vacuum, just as in the absence of willpower there will always be temptation. In both cases, the subtle voices of Chaos are magnified.

Not too long after taking administrative control of the system and repurposing several frigates, two cruisers and a battle-barge to our needs, my Mystai warned me of a disturbance in the warp.

'It is not just a ship, Grand Master, or a fleet,' Lord Cypher informed me on the bridge of my new flagship. 'This flotilla breaks the storm like a hammer on stone, with brute force.'

We readied the fleet to greet these newcomers and within days the sizeable flotilla broke warp over a matter of hours. The close arrival and coherent disposition of the ships gave me suspicion, for even in clement warp conditions it is all but impossible for one ship to stay in contact with another. Amidst the tumult that befouled the Zaramund approaches I thought it miraculous.

I again consulted with the psykers of the Mystai. Bear in mind that I had not spoken of the powers of the warp with them, though I think that the gift they possessed must at some point have told them of my burgeoning connection to the Realm of Chaos.

'Most unusual,' the Lord Cypher agreed. 'The fleet must contain a very powerful psyker, several it is likely, to exert any control over the storms. And they probably are not allies of the Emperor.'

This followed my own line of thought and we waited for the reports from the system monitor ships. Six vessels in all translated into Zaramund, all of them showing heavy signs of battle damage.

'They are here for the shipyard,' I decided, when I gathered my council to me, such as it was – Griffayn and Astelan had accompanied the fleet in preparation for the battle that never occurred. 'We cannot let them have it.'

'They are Legion vessels, cruiser class and above,' Griffayn informed me. 'A close match to our own fleet.'

'But they are war-torn, their threat is far less than their manifest would boast,' Astelan countered. 'A swift counter-attack would probably break them within hours.'

'Not without losses,' I replied. 'I know that we came to Zaramund ready for war, but let us not start one if we do not need to. We cannot know if other ships are on their way.'

'It seems that more are coming,' said Lord Cypher. 'Certainly the warp is awash with more activity than can be justified by the arrival of just six ships. That number again and more may still be en route.'

'That settles my mind,' I announced. 'Make all preparations to attack if needed, but do not provoke them. Let us first find out who has visited our new territories.'

Surveyor data later revealed the force to belong to the XIV Legion, Mortarion's Death Guard. Griffayn and the others had brought news that the Death Guard were among those numbered as Horus' allies, and one of the staunchest. I had no desire to be a lackey of Mortarion or Horus any more than the Lion and the Emperor, and here was my force in its freshly painted livery of the First Legion. It seemed battle was inevitable until the identifiers for the lead ship were checked with our knowledge banks.

It was the *Terminus Est*, flagship of Captain Calas Typhon, returned to Zaramund and my company as though by the warp gods themselves. And perhaps he was.

After establishing that it was indeed still Calas in command, I invited him to bring his ships to the dockyards and to come aboard the *Faithful Servant* – I cannot overstate the irony of the former Imperial Fists battle-barge's name.

I greeted him and his second, Vioss, at the landing bay. They wore Tactical Dreadnought armour – warsuits that dwarfed even the plate of the regular legionaries. The years had not been kind, for both showed the signs of war and hurried maintenance upon their gear, and their skin was sallow and lifeless, almost like that of a corpse.

'You must ready your fleet, Luther, an enemy is at our backs,' Calas said before even a word of greeting. 'He has pursued us relentlessly across a score of star systems.'

'Who is this pursuer?' I asked.

'Corswain,' replied Vioss. His voice was a slurred hiss, the right side of his jaw home to a pus-filled wound. 'We thought we had him at Argeus, but he turned from quarry to hunter.'

Griffayn and the others had told me that Corswain had been made seneschal to the Lion after the Legion's battles with the Night Lords across Thramas, and had tangled several times with my guest and his ships.

'He is following you here?' I asked quickly, remembering the other ships in the warp. 'This is all of your fleet?'

'Days away, at most,' said Calas. 'We must make our repairs urgently and be ready to confront him.'

'I'm not sure,' said Vioss. 'Even with the Zaramund ships, we may not have enough to fight.'

'Do not presume assets that are not yours, captain,' I said quietly.

Vioss frowned at me, a most ugly expression that flaked skin from his face. He clearly was not well, which made me uneasy. Any contagion that could affect a Space Marine would be very unwelcome in my fleet.

'Are you denying us, Luther?' the Death Guard said heavily. His breath stank and I stepped away, trying not to be intimidated.

'I deny nothing, and accept nothing,' I told him flatly. 'Unless you wish to face Corswain *and* my ships, keep your tone civil, captain.'

I turned to Calas and smiled.

'We have a little time to strategise,' I said to him, waving a hand towards the flight bay door. 'My quarters are a better venue for such discussions, and I have others that should participate. Perhaps I can return the gift of liquid consolation for your current vexatious situation?'

Vioss shifted in agitation but Calas nodded his agreement, realising the tentative offer in my words.

So I summoned Astelan, Griffayn and the Lord Cypher to my quarters and met them there with the two Death Guard. Griffayn and the new Lord Cypher required introduction, which I made briefly, and then Calas apprised us of the situation as concisely as he could.

'I need a port,' he said plainly. 'Horus' forces are gathering for the final strike towards Terra and a long-delayed rendezvous with my genefather is imminent. Yet I cannot free myself from this stubborn Dark Angel on my shoulder.'

'Why not reunite with the rest of your Legion fleet?' asked Griffayn. 'You'd have more than enough ships.'

'They are participating in affairs that I would prefer to avoid,' said Calas. His enigmatic reply was not enough for Astelan, though.

'What sort of affairs? If you want our help, you need to be open about everything,' said my First Master.

Calas turned his gaze on me, expectantly.

'If you could leave me a moment to speak with Captain Typhon alone,' I said, looking at our companions. 'Vioss, please apprise Astelan of your immediate requirements and we shall see what can be arranged.'

The Death Guard looked to his superior and received a nod of consent. Astelan seemed like he might argue but withdrew with the others, leaving me alone with Calas.

'There are bonds you dare not break, Luther,' he said sharply. 'Promises exchanged, of duty and brotherhood.'

'And yet where have you and Erebus been these last decades?' I replied harshly, unwilling to be upbraided in my own chamber. 'What have you given Caliban except silence?'

'Did you ever call upon us? Did you use the herald that we sent?' he asked.

I remembered that first encounter with the nephilla, the thought that it had been waiting for me.

'I see you realise your error,' said Calas. 'We were ever ready for your word. It seems you have done well without us, all the same.'

'A ship!' I cried, a trifle more dramatically than I had intended. The utterance of it made plain my own short-sightedness, expunging my frustration. 'Just one ship was all I needed, if I had but asked…'

'You may not have called on us, but now I call upon you, Luther,' Calas said evenly. 'My foe is your foe, and in recognition of our mutuality I need you to fight beside me.'

The rest went unspoken, the consequences should I break our bond.

'Let me speak to my council and work out what can be done,' I said to him, extending a conciliatory hand.

He did not shake it, but stood, towering over me in his immense battleplate.

'I await your communication,' he said before heading towards the door.

I despatched Griffayn to escort them back to their ship, while taking counsel from Lord Cypher and Astelan. It was no surprise to find them at cross purposes.

'You must make alliance with the Death Guard,' the Lord Cypher insisted. 'If Corswain finds us here, retribution will surely follow. Our presence is in direct defiance of the Lion's edict.'

'I think Corswain has far more pressing matters, Sar Luther,' said Astelan, helping himself to the wine I had poured for Calas and Vioss, which sat on the table untouched. 'The Death Guard give us good reason to hold Zaramund, which we of course have seized to ensure it remains as a transit point for the Emperor's forces.'

Neither knew of my deeper links to Calas, and the pact we

had made with the powers as our witnesses. And both spoke as they believed. To court Corswain risked becoming dragged back into the Legion, all hope of Caliban's independence dashed to pieces. But to fire upon Dark Angels ships was a declaration of our deceit and intent that would reverberate across the galaxy. The Lion would hear in time and he would respond.

'It seems we have been placed as a fulcrum of this war more swiftly than I imagined,' I told them. 'As it always is, to make ally with one side is to make enemy with the other.'

'We have broken from the Lion, the Dark Angels are already our enemies,' the Lord Cypher said.

'The *Lion* is our foe,' countered Astelan. 'Not the entire Legion. He has been split from Corswain for years. He might not even live, for all that we know, or is trapped in the east with Guilliman for bad company. If we befriend Corswain, we increase our power. On the other hand, Captain Typhon did not mention the Legion fleet by accident, but as a reminder of coming power. I do not think chance brought him to Zaramund, but a rendezvous. Mortarion and his fleet will be here, sooner or later. Your past is with Typhon, not Mortarion. I do not think the primarch will be so keen to negotiate with Dark Angels.'

'Your argument works both ways,' I replied, exasperated by the pair of them, but myself even more. 'Corswain's head would make a valuable bargaining chip with Mortarion. We need the goodwill of Calas to support us if we do run afoul of the Death Guard primarch.'

I held up my hand to silence them as both made to continue, wishing time to think a little longer. And it was time well spent, for a few minutes later it seemed the obvious answer came to me.

'I refuse this dichotomy,' I said to them. 'Caliban is powerful on its own or not at all. This civil war is nothing to us – we cannot afford to alienate either side, nor court them.'

'But what of the two fleets?' said Astelan. 'Practicality must trump principle. The Death Guard are here and Corswain is coming. Whichever prevails between them will come for us next, and it is likely to be Corswain by the account of Vioss and Typhon.'

'There will be no battle,' I said, taking the wine glass from him. I emptied it with a single mouthful. 'There is another way to settle this. Lord Cypher, how long until Corswain's fleet arrives?'

He did not reply immediately, and the slight drop in the chamber's temperature suggested that he communed with the other Mystai by strange means.

'Such matters are not precise, but even with fair currents it will be at least twelve hours before their first ships break warp,' he told me. 'If Typhon and his ships turn back now, they would not reach the Mandeville point for another thirteen hours after that.'

'Corswain cannot hope that his fleet will arrive in any coherent formation,' added Astelan. His experience in void warfare far outmatched mine, so I was happy to hear his opinion. 'A commander's greatest fear is running into a prepared enemy guarding the translation point. Every time he jumps after Typhon he risks ambush, so he must be pretty confident of overwhelming force once his entire fleet arrives, able to handle a few early losses while the others gather.'

'But if we add our–' began Lord Cypher, but I had already made my intent clear and cut him off.

'There will be no battle at Zaramund,' I told them again, more insistently. 'I will contact Calas directly while you make the arrangements I am about to tell you. We have twelve hours to hide the Death Guard fleet.'

The captain of the XIV took some convincing. He was trusting me with quite a feat, so I cannot lay any blame for his persistent questioning. Eventually, I was able to persuade him that my course of action was the only one with any good surety of success. Any attempt to engage the Dark Angels risked calamity for us both, while Corswain's imminent arrival made any attempt to get the Death Guard out of the Zaramund System unachievable within the likely timeframe. I made it clear that I was already guilty of a terrible collusion by not attacking as soon as Calas' fleet arrived, which gave him some assurance that whatever happened our fates were entwined and I worked to our mutual best interest.

My plan was straightforward enough in theory. The Death Guard would power down their systems to minimum and drift in the void, virtually invisible. My story to Corswain would be that Calas arrived, we skirmished briefly, before he escaped back into the warp. To seal the deception, we would destroy one of his smallest ships, creating some debris and energy residue that spoke of an exchange of fire.

It was a lot to achieve in twelve hours, because distances across space are vast and vessels the size of the *Terminus Est* do not suddenly kill their power output in minutes. In the end, nineteen hours passed before the first ship of Corswain's fleet translated in-system, and it was another seven after that until Corswain's flagship broke warp. We had hailed the first arrivals to assure them of the friendship of the system but they were understandably distrustful of voxmitted signals, even though we still had the Legion codes. I needed to speak to Corswain directly and was able to do so shortly after his ship dropped in-system.

I am sure you can imagine his shock at seeing my face appear on the vid-link, his surprise even greater than Calas'.

'*Luther!*' he declared, eyes widening.

I admit to certain callous devilry at that moment, having the advantage of greater preparedness.

'Seneschal Corswain, I may have been compelled to Caliban

but I do not recall being stripped of my title,' I snapped back, and in one simple move had gained the momentum of the conversation.

'Apologies, Sar Luther,' Corswain replied, now further disconcerted by his failure of decorum. 'My surprise has ambushed my manners.'

I tried to remember what I could of Corswain, and what Belath, Griffayn and others had told me of the legionary who had become de facto leader of the Legion in the Lion's absence. Obedient, diligent and utterly dedicated to the Lion's last command to him: to engage the enemy wherever possible. It was important to maintain the initiative in our discussion so that more awkward questions did not arise.

'I am very glad to see you, so soon after our episode with the Death Guard,' I said to him. Best to put the subject front and centre than give the approach of any dissembling. Surely if I was so keen to bring up the subject I had nothing to hide?

'You confirm that the Death Guard were here?' Corswain asked.

I felt a little thrill of delight at his phrasing. In the past tense; he already assumed that Calas and his ships were no longer here. It was then that my confidence became overconfidence, for my mouth ran away from my brain a little.

'I would be happy to send you our scan records of their fleet – they were in quite some poor repair, Sar Corswain,' I offered enthusiastically, cursing myself even as the last syllables left my lips. I tried to counter my own direction of travel immediately. 'Though I would not wish to delay you here any longer than necessary.'

'Delay?' exclaimed Corswain. 'No, Sar Luther, we can make use of a little time here, if your lighters are ready to move supplies to the outer system for us.'

In the uttering of those words my apprehension became grave misgiving: for every minute Corswain's fleet remained in the system, the greater the likelihood that the Death Guard would be discovered. Even so, there was nothing more I could say without raising suspicion.

'Of course,' I told the seneschal. 'Ships are already on their way.'

'*Good,*' said Corswain. I thought he was going to cut the link but he did not. After a few seconds he continued. '*It has been a long time, Sar Luther. You would be most welcome to join me aboard the* Wrath's Descent. *We have a great deal to discuss.*'

I was just formulating a polite decline to the offer when Corswain's expression hardened and he leaned closer to the lens of his vidcaster.

'*For instance, Sar Luther, I am very eager to hear why it is that you are at Zaramund and not still on Caliban as commanded,*' he said sternly.

I felt like I had been slapped, his tone not accusing, but certainly one used to address a subordinate. I thought him an over-promoted Paladin, but I was mistaken. I understood then that Corswain had grown well into his rank, and truly I was no longer second in the eyes of the Legion.

The Death Guard were of no use, dormant and defenceless, so I had to continue the performance as long as possible.

'My pleasure, Sar Corswain,' I replied.

To comply with the necessity of meeting Corswain in person I moved the *Faithful Servant* out to his fleet with the victualling flotilla. Astelan and Lord Cypher were both repetitive in their attempts to discuss the manoeuvre with me, but I gave them no time for audience. I was in no mood to entertain their distracting politics. There was another there that I could not rightly refuse, however.

Typhon had insisted on being aboard during the subterfuge, having despatched Vioss back to the *Terminus Est*. I alone knew of his presence, for he was hidden in my quarters. I was in no doubt that should anything go awry, the First Captain of the Death Guard would ensure I suffered ill consequences before any other, and he had made it clear that he had particular pacts with powers of which we were mutually aware to see his will enacted even after death.

It felt ignominious to once again be second player, treated like an inferior by warriors that should have held me as their equal but did not simply because I was not as surgically altered as them. Their physical superiority automatically created within their minds a certainty of moral and intellectual superiority that was undeserved. It was this inequality that had in part driven me to even the balance with the aid of the warp.

'Heed my warning, Luther,' Calas told me when I relayed to him my need to meet Corswain in person. 'Whether from this realm or the next, I will avenge myself against any who has broken oaths to be my brother. I am becoming something far greater than what you see, and you too can harness that power.'

I had some inkling of what he meant from my studies and practices, hesitant though they had been. The warp was energy unlimited, if one could tap into it the correct way. I had focused on minor sorceries, small tricks of the mind to distract or persuade, as well as honing my summoning. Yet I had glimpsed the magnitude of the power that was there to grasp if one was willing to risk all.

'Your threats are redundant,' I told him. 'If Corswain suspects anything then my life is already forfeit, and any admittance to my collusion would end with similarly bad consequences. I am already fearful of his mood regarding my departure from Caliban and can only hope that pragmatism and immediate necessity erase any desire for further censure.'

'There are worse fates than death,' he told me grimly. 'And after death too…'

I absorbed this in silence. Calas said nothing, but appeared in deep thought, or perhaps listening to some voice to which I was deaf. After a few seconds, the First Captain's mood lightened.

'You think that the powers I speak of are distant, but they are not, Luther,' Calas assured me. 'They wait for you, eager to have you as their champion. One act of dedication, a true acknowledgement of your allegiance, will set free your nascent potency.'

He presented me with a dagger, sized for a legionary but not too big for my grasp. The handle was rusted metal, the blade shimmering like an oil slick, not quite present. I did not take it at first, until he stepped forward and pressed it into my palm. My gloved fingers closed around the handle and it felt cold in my grasp.

'This blade can slay anything,' the Death Guard said solemnly. 'It is a lifebane, deadly against even a warrior of the Legiones Astartes. Perhaps even a primarch. Alone with Corswain, one thrust and you will signal the powers of the warp of your undying devotion. The act will not go unprotected nor unrewarded. There are greater things than starships in the void of space. As all eyes draw towards Terra, let them alight on you for a brief moment and the future of Caliban will be assured.'

I took the proffered sheath for the blade, which seemed plain enough, and strapped it to my belt. Looking at the dagger one more time, holding back my revulsion, I considered his words. Slipping the knife into its home, I nodded my acquiescence.

'We stand upon the brink of greatness,' Calas declared, lifting a fist to his chest. 'Know that Horus is only the key to unlocking the gates of immortality, he need not be your master. The powers we serve would have us each do as we desire, freed from slavery not indentured to another false lord.'

I found his words reassuring, and we spoke for the remaining time before the rendezvous on the nature of those powers and my own observations around them. He was forthcoming at times, oddly reticent at others, but in the hours we passed on the journey to the *Wrath's Descent* I renewed both our friendship and my dedication to our shared cause.

I left Astelan in command of the ship, trusting him just a little more than the Lord Cypher. Neither was really in any position to betray me, for the same reasons I could not turn traitor on Calas. All of us were guilty of a conspiracy against the Lion, the Emperor and the Legion, and all would be found equally guilty in the eyes of the seneschal.

I was escorted to Corswain's quarters, not so much under suspicion but certainly treated as a wayward cousin who might wander again. I still had my sword and pistol with me, and the lifebane, so they did not consider me a physical threat. However, my welcome from the seneschal was equally stiff.

'I do not know the details of why you were sent to Caliban from Sarosh,' he began, without even a greeting. 'I do know that when you were returned there after the campaign in this system, the Lion was most explicit in his compulsion against you.'

He offered no seat or drink, though there were both in his quarters. Seeing him in full regalia was an imposing sight, with the pelt of a Calibanite beast across one shoulder, his plate much marked in battle, his skin scarred like chipped stone rather than flesh. There was an energy about him that was very potent, and reminded me much of the Lion when he was keeping his frustration in check.

On a screen behind him was a display I recognised immediately as the Zaramund System. It was a live-feed from the strategium. A subpanel showed the dispositions of my battle-barge and the resupply lighters and I assumed the ever-increasing detail on the main screen was accumulating surveyor data from the fleet.

How long until one of the Dark Angels vessels detected something amiss: either a Death Guard ship floating in the void or one of my transports hidden among the many civilian vessels in and around the main shipyard?

I was about to begin my answer, which I had prepared and rehearsed with myself several times, when he continued, a note of anger entering his voice.

'More importantly, I would know why you denied me the ships and warriors I needed,' he growled. He turned and pointed to the system schematic on the wall. 'I see among your fleet the *Spear of Truth* but have had no word from Belath. Where are my damn reinforcements, Luther?'

I felt the coldness of the lifebane at my hip, but knew I could not yet strike. Even with his back to me, Corswain would sense my attack before it landed, and I would be dead within moments. I recalled that he was one of the Legion's greatest bladesmen, and I was long out of practice.

I had not expected to be confronted quite so forcefully, but I did not allow doubt to enter my thoughts. I replied smoothly, as though my interrogation was entirely natural and deserved, but of little concern. I knew that this was a difficult moment, one which at best might see me stripped of my command and my ships, and at worst would end with my death. If I was to retain both lifeblood and resources, I had to spin a tale better than any other before.

'The warp is a dangerous place, and journeys across it are uncertain,' I said, which was of no novelty to Corswain as I could see from his deepening frown reflected on the screen. 'Though Belath came to me with the ships, it was after a voyage fraught with terrible encounters and setbacks as only a veteran of Caliban can imagine. A quest of the most legendary kind.'

As I spoke my natural animation returned but I was careful not to over-elaborate, lest I be caught out in the lie later. Always bear as close to the truth as possible, changing the least to make events fit your own narrative.

'We welcomed news of the continuing war and set about preparing the embarkation of your reinforcements. Before the ships set out we were in a terrible quandary.' I dredged my memory for pertinent details to sprinkle through the fabrication. 'Belath had departed from Argeus but we had no reliable information of your movements afterwards. It seemed unwise to send out the transports fully laden with warriors but with no certain destination. They were as likely to run into foe as friend, more likely it seemed. We needed to find some way to gain a bearing on your whereabouts. Astropaths are no good in this storm, so we thought perhaps we needed genuine sightings. An armada does not pass through a system without remark.'

I left the explanation open, an invitation for Corswain to speak. If he asked further questions I was in a rough tangle, but if he accepted what I had said, I foresaw easier riding ahead.

'You came to Zaramund to look for me?' he said, both asking a question and accepting my account as he turned back to me. I was still in the depths of the woods but now I could see several paths out.

'It seemed a logical place to start, given its proximity to both Argeus and Caliban,' I said evenly, meeting his gaze for a few seconds. 'When the Death Guard arrived I feared we had made a terrible misjudgement, putting ourselves directly into harm's way. Yet your imminent arrival no doubt spared us the worst of their attentions.'

Corswain replied only with a grunt and returned to his study of the system scans. I wondered if there was something there that already betrayed me and he was simply luring me into a self-confession.

I took a couple of paces closer, nonchalant, and still not yet close enough to attack with confidence. I trusted that his armour would be no barrier to the insubstantial lifebane, but needed to be absolutely certain he could not dodge the blow. The moment I thought he disbelieved me, I would have to make my move, for there would be no time if he regarded me as a threat.

'I cannot see the transports,' Corswain said quietly. 'Do I need to travel to Caliban to fetch my legionaries?'

'They are not here,' I answered, eluding the question as best I could. I advanced another couple of strides, my hand moving to the hilt of the lifebane. Its weight dragged at me, making me acutely aware of its presence. Now I was sure I could strike the deadly blow. Beyond the Space Marine's bulk the screen continued to fill with runes and notations, as data flooded through the systems of the *Wrath's Descent*. I knew vaguely where the Death Guard were hiding, spread out to avoid detection, and the joint surveyor boundary was creeping ever closer.

I realised that it was a matter of hours if not minutes before they would be discovered. The plan would fail.

'I can see that they are not here,' said the seneschal.

He started to turn.

Now was my moment. The blade in my hand, driving towards his midriff under the arm. Seal the pact and embrace the powers of the warp.

Yet instead I lifted my hand from the hilt and crossed my arms. I would not plunge into that bargain on such terms, cornered and afraid. If I had wanted to wage war on the Dark Angels I would have sided with Calas and attacked without need for infernal assistance.

My wits and my words had always served me well, and to them I turned rather than rely on the vagaries of the warp.

'You can see that our facilities are ready to provide refit before you continue to Terra,' I said amiably, stepping past the giant warrior. I made a few adjustments, concentrating the view on the docks around Zaramund itself, and lifted a finger to indicate open dock spars on the screen. 'Had I known you were coming we could have cleared more space.'

'What refit?' Corswain looked at the screen and then back to me, searching for an answer.

'I assumed you would be continuing after the traitors,' I said, feigning confusion. 'Horus has gathered his forces for the last attack. The transports will be coming from Caliban, of course, now we are sure Zaramund is safe. It might take some time, with the storms, and there are enemy flotillas everywhere.'

Corswain's eyes narrowed and I wondered if he sensed my misdirection. It was time to seal my fate, one way or the other, and I drew on everything I had learned about the seneschal. Loyal and obedient, but his greatest desire would be to reunite with his primarch.

'I would be sure the Lion makes all speed for the defence of the Throneworld, if not there already,' I continued. 'I know I have been out of favour for a long while, but I was his gain-brother, nobody knows him better than I do. He would not shun an opportunity to confront Horus directly.'

I could see Corswain's gaze slide back to the screen, his expression calculating, lips moving a little in thought. I resisted the temptation to speak further. Sometimes you need to let your opponent think their way into the position you desire rather than forcing the issue. It was as if I could track the internal debate with each flick of his gaze and clench of his jaw, first one way and then the other.

'We do not have time for refit, the enemy could be at Terra already,' he said eventually.

When you have your opponent where you want, give them no room to escape but also be certain they will not change their mind.

'I cannot say how soon the reinforcements will arrive,' I said, spreading my hands in apology. 'The moment they do, I will lead them to Terra myself.'

I tried not to tense. Had I gone too far? Would the reminder of the reinforcements persuade him to stay longer?'

No. He would sooner lose a limb than be delayed any longer than necessary, now that I had laid before him the dual prospect of reuniting with the Lion and confronting Horus' attack. Even so, I needed insurance that he would not surprise me again. A thought occurred to me as I watched the flickering runes on the display panel.

'One of my Librarians has something of a talent for reading the warp,' I said. 'Vassago. It was he that foresaw your arrival and forecast Typhon's departure for Terra.'

'Typhon?' Corswain said sharply, focusing on me. I realised my misstep and tried to stay calm. As I've said before, it takes a very cool nerve to lie to a Space Marine. One's biology has a tendency towards betrayal. I was again aware of the icy touch of the lifebane at my waist. Riskier than before, but it was there if I needed it. Just as I tried to make no indication of guilt, I was acutely aware of making no movement that might appear hostile. Corswain would react before thought, as would any Space Marine.

'Our readings picked up a vessel that I recognised as the *Terminus Est*,' I explained languidly, forcing a smile. 'I regarded her captain as an ally in happier times, in this same star system.'

'Yes, of course,' said Corswain. He scrutinised me for several seconds. The lifebane's chill touch throbbed against my skin. 'You fought beside Typhon here.'

'Vassago,' I repeated. 'He may be of help tracking the enemy to Terra. At least, another warp seer would not be a burden, I hope. And of course, take such warriors from my ship as I can spare, to bolster your own strength.'

'Whatever assistance you can give,' said Corswain, but he was already distracted, his thoughts moving away from Zaramund to a far more important confrontation. I could see he was now eager for me to be gone, the lure of glory at Terra and the call to action thrumming along his warrior nerves.

'I will send what forces I can spare,' I assured him. He grunted his assent and turned to the screen, presenting his broad back for a final time.

'I will have you escorted back to your gunship,' he said.

In a few seconds the doors would open and there would be no chance to use the lifebane. I had engineered a fragile solution, but still the promise of Calas lingered in my thoughts. A sign of my devotion. The unleashing of my potential. The favour of dark gods. There was a life beyond this moment to consider.

All I desired could be mine with a single stroke of a blade.

I turned and walked to the door, bidding Corswain farewell.

'What became of the lifebane?' demanded Nahariel. 'And what has this to do with Alldric?'

Luther had relaxed during his telling, having moved to his knees like a supplicant. He looked up, as if seeing the Supreme Grand Master for the first time, so lost had he been in his recollection.

'The lifebane? I kept it. I kept it close, for when I knew I would need it. For when I would face a foe I could not beat any other way.'

'You speak of the Lion?' snapped Nahariel. 'You used this sorcerous assassin's weapon to slay the primarch!'

'I did not kill him,' Luther insisted, rocking back and forward slowly. The image formed as he held out his hand, black against the skin of his palm. He heard the crack of guns and hoarse shouts. The ire of the Lion boring into him, even as a blade that had slain kings jutted from Luther's midriff. 'It was there, at my waist, when the Lion put his sword through me. But I could not draw it. I looked into that mask of rage and knew that I had been wrong.'

Luther started to sob, reliving his folly, the breath of his gain-brother in his nostrils mixed with blood. He almost choked on the words.

'The gods still wanted me to make a final sacrifice. But I was always for Caliban, never for them, and I could not slay my gain-brother any more than I could strike down faithful Corswain.'

'And Alldric? Tell me how I find him, how to stop him.'

'Why?' Luther's shoulders flexed as he cried, and he sank forward, forehead pressed against the hard floor. 'Why do you not hear me?'

'Speak clearly and I will hear your confession,' said Nahariel.

'The scenery changes but your road always heads in the same direction, no matter what I say!' snarled Luther, sitting up, face flushed with anger. 'I warn you again and again, but you ignore me.'

He rose to his feet, arms held up, imploring.

'This is my torment! Oh, to be an icon of falsehood that sees the truth, it is a punishment too far, I say. Release me, Lion of the Forest! I cannot save your sons! I cannot do what you need of me.'

'It is not the Dark Angels that need salvation,' rasped Nahariel before he stormed from the room.

'Come back to them,' Luther whispered to the growing shadows, the gleam of red eyes within. 'Bring him back! Release him... He will be the salvation of us all.'

TALE OF THE HEART

The aggressive mood of his interrogators returned, so that the matter of Luther's confession occupied them more than any intelligence they might glean from his fractured prophecies. Sometimes they used words, sometimes they used blades or fists. Neither worked, for Luther cared little for pain of the body. The torture he underwent during his stasis sleep was far more painful, to have a slow, eked-out sensation of damnation.

He tried so hard to make them see that it was not him that needed to repent. The words never seemed to come out straight. Perhaps that was the true curse the gods had placed upon him for his betrayal. One that had been so gifted at diplomacy and statecraft now mangled every thought with his traitor tongue.

Then one came that was different again.

Azrael he was called, and there was an energy about him that settled Luther. He was calm where others had been defiant. Cautious of Luther, and not sympathetic, but understanding of the manic nature of his existence. He spoke as much as he listened, telling Luther how much time had passed and snippets of news from the outside world, all the better to centre his thoughts on the present.

Yet even then it was hard to stay cogent. The more Luther dwelt on what he had become, and what the Dark Angels had turned into, the more desperate he became for his release. And so the cycle continued unabated.

After several encounters with Azrael, Luther came to his senses on his knees, hands clasped in front of him, filled with a sense of deep need. He had been begging forgiveness again, but still the Lion did not answer. Instead Azrael stood before him, his face grimmer than any Supreme Grand Master before.

He had not said a word before a memory came to Luther and he began to speak, knowing in his heart it was what the leader of the Dark Angels needed to hear, but knowing he would also never listen.

I grew up in these stone walls. These towers, the Angelicasta, great Aldurukh about it. I hear the walls speaking, of all the cruel and glad and beautiful and ugly things they have seen. They have been ripped from their home as I was.

A child in this place. A child of the Order. Proud knights, high walls and tales of beast-slaying were my upbringing. I learned to speak and wield sword and ride without ever leaving the outer walls. I loved and grieved here, for dead parents, and cried over my lost wife and child. I have laughed and sobbed, betrayed and known betrayal, with the name of Aldurukh in my thoughts.

This place knows me even better than the Lion.

And it is still here, eternal. The bastion of the Order. Fortress of the Dark Angels. Their strength given form.

This is the first occasion I have recalled this memory in all my time alive, but it is as stark now as the day it happened.

When I was but seven years old as the chroniclers of Terra count the days, I awoke one night from a frightening dream. I lay in my chamber as starlight streamed through the window and thought I heard a noise from without the door.

I left my bed and opened the door to investigate. There was something strange about the wards and dorms, a silence lay about the place. No breath or snore or creak seemed to disturb the tower where my family lived. But I did not feel afraid.

Barefoot, I padded along the stone passageway to the stairwell and started to descend.

I became aware of being observed, but no matter where I looked I saw nobody. Again, this was not fear-inspiring, it was simply a reality. I kept going down the steps, further than I thought possible, beyond any hall or kitchen or quarters I had known.

Light suffused the air around me, for I had brought no torch but encountered no darkness.

I came upon a great wooden door bound in metal, as tall as a wall gate. I thought myself in a dream, but everything was very real. The air that misted in my breath, the prickle of my skin, the weight of the door as I pushed it open.

A flurry of movement drew my eye and I saw my first Watcher in the Dark. Red eyes gleaming, it became one with the shadows, but not before I followed, slipping between the door and arch.

I realised I had dreamed this before, but this time I was no longer asleep. In my dreams I had been taken with a sensation of menace, desperate to awake, but now I felt a welcome, a silent song calling me onwards. There was warmth, not cold, and I hurried forward, eager.

My course took me through passages and rough tunnels, across caves of glittering strata and natural columns, into the very foundations of Aldurukh it seemed, but I spied not another soul on my travel. I knew I was lost, but that it did not matter for what I sought lay ahead, not behind.

Then another Watcher appeared, in the distance ahead, and I felt fear returning. I slowed, uncertain, but did not stop. I wanted to see what was beyond the next archway, a portal of total blackness. More Watchers came before me, glaring with crimson gaze, and I faltered even more.

Yet their challenge was an affront to me, raised on tales of the bravest knights. To know fear is to learn courage, I had been taught. The greater the dread, the bolder the hero to prevail. I wanted the warmth and welcome to return and resented the Watchers for driving it away.

Then came a hissing, on the edge of hearing, a discontent in the air itself. The Watchers thought to bar my path but they could not stand before me, becoming nothing but dark fog as I approached.

The arch of utter darkness was before me and cold terror froze my limbs at last.

'Turn back,' the whispers became. 'Turn back.'

Defiance known only in the heart of a frustrated child welled up inside me and I stepped forward.

The darkness swallowed me, but there was no cold, no fear.

I came upon a chamber suffused with pale green light, with more archways leading from it. The light came from these openings, but in one I saw a shadow. At first it was just a flicker, a momentary dimming of the light, but it grew thicker and darker as I watched.

The shadow became a thread, became a tendril, became a serpentine limb blindly questing along the tunnel towards me. I wanted to see what the limb looked like, but equally I wanted to run. Caught between curiosity and terror, I stood rooted to the spot and closed my eyes.

I felt a draught and warmth, and then I opened my eyes

again and found myself in a hall not far from my room. Red eyes glimmered for a split second in the shadows around the walls before I was alone once more. Dazed, I found my way back to my room, fell upon my cot and into a dreamless sleep.

All of Caliban is destroyed yet it lives on. It is here, in this place, in your hearts.

Luther broke from the dream-vision and found himself alone. As he suspected, his warning had gone unheeded, Azrael had departed. It seemed that the sound of his apocalyptic visions haunted the edge of hearing – flames crackling, blade striking blade, the report of weapons and shouts of the warriors that bore them.

As he waited for the moment to subside or the thought-drift to consume him, Luther examined his surrounds. He saw no shadows save for the natural darkness cast by the flickering torches in their sconces. No watchful eyes of red in deeper darkness.

The door was still open.

Stasis had not returned.

He smelled smoke. Taking a deeper breath he assured himself that it was real and not imagined. With focus came a similar certainty regarding the sounds of battle close at hand. The Rock was under attack, his captors distracted.

The door was still open.

Luther's thoughts returned to it as he stretched painfully weak limbs.

Left by Azrael or opened by another?

He took a cautious step, and then another, and another.

ABOUT THE AUTHOR

Gav Thorpe's long and prolific career with Black Library has seen him write across the depth and breadth of the Warhammer universes. Author of the Horus Heresy novels *The First Wall, Deliverance Lost, Angels of Caliban, Corax,* and novella *The Lion,* he has also recently written the titles *Luther: First of the Fallen* and *Rogal Dorn: The Emperor's Crusader.* His Warhammer 40,000 work includes *Indomitus,* the Dawn of Fire novel *The Wolftime,* and the fan-favourite Last Chancers series, amongst many others. For Age of Sigmar, Gav wrote the novel *The Red Feast,* and in 2017 he won the David Gemmell Legend Award for his novel *Warbeast.* He lives and works in Nottingham.

YOUR NEXT READ

THE LION: SON OF THE FOREST
by Mike Brooks

The Lion. Son of the Emperor, brother of demigods and primarch of the Dark Angels.
Awakened. Returned. And yet… lost.

For these stories and more, go to **blacklibrary.com**, **warhammer.com**,
Games Workshop and Warhammer stores, all good book stores or visit one of the thousands of
independent retailers worldwide, which can be found at **warhammer.com/store-finder**

An extract from
The Lion: Son of the Forest
by Mike Brooks

The river sings silver notes: a perpetual, chaotic babble in which a fantastically complex melody seems to hang, tantalising, just out of reach of the listener. He could spend eternity here trying to find the heart of it, without ever succeeding, yet still not consider the time wasted. The sound of water over stone, the interplay of energy and matter, creates a quiet symphony that is both unremarkable and unique. He does not know how long he has been here, just listening.

Nor, he realises, does he know where *here* is.

The listener becomes aware of himself in stages, like a sleeper passing from the deepest, darkest depths of slumber, through the shallows of semi-consciousness where thought swirls in confusing eddies, and then into the light. First comes the realisation that he is not the song of the river; that he is in fact separate from it, and listening to it. Then sensation dawns, and he realises he is sitting on the river's bank. If there is a sun, or suns, then he cannot see them through the branches of the trees overhead and the mist that hangs heavily in the air, but there is still light enough for him to make out his surroundings.

The trees are massive, and mighty, with great trunks that could not be fully encircled by one, two, perhaps even half a dozen people's outstretched arms. Their rough, cracked bark pockmarks them with shadows, as though the trees themselves are camouflaged. The ground beneath their branches is fought over by tough shrubs: sturdy, twisted, thorny things strangling each other in the contest for space and light, like children unheeded at the feet of adults. The earth in which they grow is dark and rich, and when the listener digs his fingers into it, it smells of life, and death, and other things besides. It is a familiar smell, although he cannot say from where, or why.

His fingers, he realises as they penetrate the ground, are armoured. His whole body is armoured, in fact, encased in a great suit of black plates with the faintest hint of dark green. This is a familiar sensation, too. The armour feels like a part of him – an extension, as natural as the shell of any crustacean that might lurk in the nooks and crannies of the river in front of him. He leans forward and peers down into the still water next to the bank, sheltered from the main flow by an outcropping just upstream. It becomes an almost perfect mirror surface, as smooth as a dream.

The listener does not recognise the face that looks back at him. It is deeply lined, as though a world of cares and worries has washed over it like the river water, scoring the marks of their passage into the skin. His hair is pale, streaked with blond here and there, but otherwise fading into grey and white. The lower part of his face is obscured by a thick, full beard and moustache, leaving only the lips bare; it is a distrustful mouth, one more likely to turn downwards in disapproval than quirk upwards in a smile.

He raises one hand, the fingers still smeared with dirt, before his face. The reflection does the same. This is surely his face, but the sight sparks no memory. He does not know who he is, and he does not know where he is, for all that it feels familiar.

That being the case, there seems little point in remaining here.

The listener gets to his feet, then hesitates. He cannot explain to himself why he should move, given the song of the river is so beautiful. However, the realisation of his lack of knowledge has opened something inside him, a hunger which was not there before. He will not be satisfied until he has answers.

Still, the river's song calls to him. He decides to walk along the bank, following the flow of the water and listening to it as he goes, and since he does not know where he is, one direction is as good as the other. There is a helmet on the bank, next to where he was sitting. It is the same colour as his armour, with vertical slits across the mouth, like firing slits in a wall. He picks it up, and clamps it to his waist with a movement that feels instinctual.

He does not know for how long he walks. Time is surely passing, in that one moment slips into another, and he can remember ones that came before and consider the concept of ones yet to come, but there is nothing to mark it. The light neither increases nor decreases, instead remaining an almost spectral presence which illuminates without revealing its source. Shadows lurk, but there is no indication as to what casts them. The walker is unperturbed. His eyes can pierce those shadows, just as he can smell foliage, and he can hear the river. There is no soughing of wind in the branches, for the air is still, but the moist air carries the faint hooting, hollering calls of animals of some kind, somewhere in the distance.

The river's course begins to flatten and widen. The walker follows it around a bend, then comes to a halt in shock.

On the far bank stands a building.

It is built of cut and dressed stone, a dark blue-grey rock in which brighter specks glitter. It is not immense – the surrounding trees tower over it – but it is solid. It is a castle of some kind, a fortress, intended to keep the unwanted out and whatever people and treasures lie within safe from harm. It is neither new and pristine, nor ancient and weathered. It looks as though it has always stood here, and always shall. And on the wide, calm water in front of it sits a boat.

It is small, wooden, and unpainted. It is large enough for one person, and indeed one person is sitting in it. The walker's eyes can make him out, even at distance. He is old, and not old in the same way as the walker's face is. Time has not lined his features, it has ravaged them. His cheeks are sunken, his limbs are wasted; skin that was once clearly a rich chestnut now has an ashen patina, and his long hair is lifeless, dull grey, and matted. However, that grey head supports a crown: little more than a circlet of gold, but a crown nonetheless.

In his hands, swollen of knuckle and weak of grip, he holds a rod. The line is already cast into the water. Now he sits, hunched over as though in pain, a small, ancient figure in a small, simple boat.

The walker does not stop to wonder why a king would be fishing in such a manner. He is aware of the context of such things, but he does not know from where, and they do not matter to him. Here is someone who might have some answers for him.

'Greetings!' he calls. His voice is strong, rich and deep, although rough around the edges from age or disuse, or both. It carries across the water. The old king in the boat blinks, and when his eyes open again, they are looking at the walker.

'What is this place?' the walker demands.

The old king blinks again. When his eyes open this time, they are focused on the water once more. It is as though the walker is not there at all, a dismissal of minimal effort.

The walker discovers that he is not used to being ignored, and nor does he appreciate it. He steps into the water, intending to wade across the river so the king cannot so easily dismiss him. He is unconcerned about the current: he is strong of limb, and knows without knowing that his armour is waterproof, and that should he don his helmet he will be able to breathe even if he is submerged.

He has only gone a few steps, in up to his knees, when he realises there are shadows in the water: large shadows that circle the small boat, around and around. They do not bite on the line, and nor do they capsize the craft in which the fisher sits, but either could be disastrous.

Moreover, the walker realises, the king is wounded. The walker cannot see the wound, but he can smell the blood. A rich, copperish tang tickles his nose. It is not a smell that delights him, but neither does he find it repulsive. It is simply a scent, one that he is able to parse and understand. The king is bleeding into the water, drip by drip. Perhaps that is what has drawn the shadows to this place. Perhaps they would have been here anyway.

Some of the shadows start to peel away, and head towards the walker.

The walker is not a being to whom fear comes naturally, but nor is he unfamiliar with the concept of danger. The shadows in the water are unknown to him, and move like predators.

+Come back to the bank.+

The walker whirls. A small figure stands on the land, swathed in robes of dark green, so that it nearly blends into the background against which it stands. It is the size of a child, perhaps, but the walker knows it to be something else.

It is a Watcher in the Dark.

+Come back to the bank,+ the Watcher repeats. Although its communication can hardly be called a voice – there is no sound, merely a sensation inside the walker's head that imparts meaning – it feels increasingly urgent nonetheless. The walker realises that he is not normally one to turn away from a challenge, but nor is he willing to ignore a Watcher in the Dark. It feels like a link, a connection to what came before, to what he should be able to remember.

He wades back, and steps up onto the bank. The approaching shadows hesitate for a moment, then circle away towards the king in his boat.

+They would destroy you,+ the Watcher says. The walker understands that it is talking about the shadows. There are layers to the feelings in his head now, feelings that are the mental aftertaste of the Watcher's communication. Disgust lurks there, but also fear.

'Where is this place?' the walker asks.

+Home.+

The walker waits, but nothing else is forthcoming. Moreover, he understands that there will not be. So far as the Watcher is concerned, that is not simply all the information that is required, but all that is available to give.

He looks out over the water, towards the king. The old man still sits hunched over, rod in his hands, blood leaking from his wounds one drip at a time.

'Why does he ignore me?'

+You did not ask the correct question.+

The walker looks around. The shadows in the water are still there, so it seems foolish to try to cross. However, he has seen no bridge over the river, nor another boat. He has no tools with which to build such a craft from the trees around him, and the knowledge of how to do so does not come easily to his mind. He is not like some of his brothers, for whom creation is natural…

His brothers. Who are his brothers?

Shapes flit through his mind, as ephemeral as smoke in a storm. He cannot get a grip, cannot wrestle them into anything that makes sense, or anything onto which his reaching mind can latch. The peace brought about by the song of the river is gone, and in its place is uncertainty and frustration. Nonetheless, the walker would not return to his former state. To knowingly welcome ignorance is not his way.

He catches a glimpse of something pale, a long way off through the trees, but on his side of the river. He begins to walk towards it, leaving the river behind him – he can always find it again, he knows its song – and making his way through the undergrowth. The plants are thick and verdant, but he is strong and sure. He ducks under spines, slaps aside strangling tendrils reaching out for anything that passes, and avoids breaking the twigs, which would leak sap so corrosive it might damage even his armour.

He does not wonder how he knows these things. The Watcher said that this was home.

The Watcher itself has been left behind, but it keeps reappearing, stepping out of the edge of shadows. It says nothing; not until the walker passes through a thicket of thorns and finally gets a clearer view of what he had seen.

It is a building, or at least the roof of one; that is all he can see from here. It is a dome of beautiful pale stone, supported by pillars. Whereas before he had been finding his own route through the forest, now there is a clear path ahead, a route of short grass hemmed in on either side by bushes and tree trunks. It curves away, rather than arrowing straight towards the pale building, but the walker knows that is where it leads.

+Do not take that path,+ the Watcher cautions him. +You are not yet strong enough.+

The walker looks down at this tiny creature, barely knee-high to him, then breathes deeply and rolls his shoulders within his armour. He presumes he had a youth, given he now looks old. Perhaps he was stronger then. Nonetheless, his body does not feel feeble.

+That is not the strength you will need.+

The walker narrows his eyes. 'You caution me against anything that might help me make sense of my situation. What would you have me do instead?'

+Follow your nature.+

The walker breathes in again, ready to snap an answer, for he finds he is just as ill-disposed towards being denied as he is to being ignored. However, he pauses, then sniffs.

He sniffs again.

Something is amiss.

He is surrounded by the deep, rich scent of the forest, which smells of both life and death. However, now his nose detects something else: a rancid undercurrent, something that is not merely rot or decay – for these are natural odours – but far worse, far more jarring.

Corruption.

This is something wrong, something twisted. It is something that should not be here: something that should not, in fact, exist at all.

The walker knows what he must do. He must follow his nature.

The hunter steps forward, and starts to run in pursuit of his quarry.

YOUR
NEXT READ

LAZARUS: ENMITY'S EDGE
by Gary Kloster

Across the warp storms of the Great Rift, a distress beacon calls for aid. The Rock is listening, for the Dark Angels have only their oaths to remind them of who they are.

For these stories and more, go to blacklibrary.com, warhammer.com, Games Workshop and Warhammer stores, all good book stores or visit one of the thousands of independent retailers worldwide, which can be found at warhammer.com/store-finder

YOUR NEXT READ

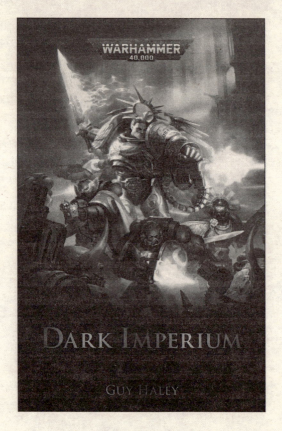

DARK IMPERIUM
by Guy Haley

The first phase of the Indomitus Crusade is over, and the conquering primarch, Roboute Guilliman, sets his sights on home. The hordes of his traitorous brother, Mortarion, march on Ultramar, and only Guilliman can hope to thwart their schemes with his Primaris Space Marine armies.

For these stories and more, go to blacklibrary.com, warhammer.com, Games Workshop and Warhammer stores, all good book stores or visit one of the thousands of independent retailers worldwide, which can be found at warhammer.com/store-finder